Gift of the Ancients

A Friend
in Need

BIANCA D'ARC

This book is a work of fiction. The names, characters, places, and incidents are products of the writer's imagination or have been used fictitiously and are not to be construed as real. Any resemblance to persons, living or dead, actual events, locale or organizations is entirely coincidental.

No part of this book may be used or reproduced in any manner whatsoever without written permission, except in the case of brief quotations embodied in critical articles and reviews.

It's a case of wrong place, right time when Hannah meets Carter in the middle of a mall shooting spree.

She's a wounded warrior...

Hannah came home from her tour in the desert with a foot busted up almost beyond repair. It's been a struggle to get back to civilian life after her injury, but she's working at the mall and doing what the doctors tell her, when all of a sudden, she's back in a firefight, in the middle of suburbia!

He's a very special operator...

Carter is tasked to look after the woman who can't run, and finds himself enchanted by her coolness under fire. He's a Special Forces warrior with a near-magic ability for language. Days after the mall incident, he feels compelled to check on her, and then, the true adventure begins as attraction explodes into heated desire, and enemies on her doorstep cause him to take drastic action.

They have a lot in common, including a smoldering mutual attraction...

Both sergeants, they're both in the Army, though under very different commands. Still, they find common ground and fiery passion, together. When a sleeper cell is awakened, it will take both of them to stop the insanity. Can they do it without losing anyone...especially each other?

DEDICATION

This book was edited and proofed during the unprecedented isolation of the Spring 2020 corona virus pandemic in the United States. Everything was made more difficult by the need for social distancing and the horrible news of illness and death bombarding us every single day. My editor, in particular, is going through a rough patch and yet, she still found time to edit this for me. Thank you, Jess, from the bottom of my heart.

I also must thank Peggy McChesney for finding a few more errors than usual. She is my final check and my dear friend for being willing to give these books a read when they might not be perfectly ready for 'human consumption.' LOL. Thank you, Peggy, for always being willing and so incredibly helpful. You're the best!

And a special nod to my 94 year old Dad, who has been putting up with my cooking for the last five weeks, while we've been in self-imposed isolation. Our small county on Long Island, in New York, is number two in the nation for corona virus illness and death right now. It's a scary place to be, especially since he is so vulnerable. (Though, I'm no spring chicken either, these days!)

Dad and I started isolating before any of the orders went out because I can't take chances with his health. As a result, we've had to eat my lousy cooking for five weeks already, and I can't tell you how much we are both looking forward to being able to eat out again!

And finally, just a thought for us all who are living through this crisis, and all those who didn't make it. My heart goes out to you and your families. We're all in this together...but at a safe, socially-distanced space. We'll get through this and when we do, I hope and pray that life will be better than ever, and all the more precious for what we have just experienced. Hang in there.

I hope this story will bring you all a little respite from your cares and woes, if only for a few hours...

PROLOGUE

Carter was back on Plum Island, doing PT with the rest of his unit. They were a top-secret military Spec Ops unit that had gone to the Middle East and come back...changed. They'd encountered something odd in that desert, and their fates had been altered by what could only have been a magical being that they met in a tower that couldn't possibly be where it had been. At least, not in the present day.

The jury was still out on whether they'd been transported back to the days of ancient Babylon or if they'd someone crossed over some interdimensional portal, but they all agreed, they'd climbed that tower and met a very strange man in the top chamber. A man wearing a turban and brightly colored clothing like something out of an *Arabian Nights* fantasy.

He'd asked them many questions about current events in the world, as if he had no idea what had been going on in the region for centuries.

Oddly, they'd answered his questions and talked with the man far longer than should have been safe for them to linger. It felt like something had compelled them to stay and chat, when they should have been on the move. The strange man had looked at each member of the unit, as if assessing them for their true character. Then, he'd smiled, and after a few more words, they had left.

It wasn't until later that they realized they had each acquired some freaky new abilities. Carter's friend, Jeff, for instance. He'd started seeing the future.

They hadn't really believed in any of it at first, but over the next few days, working as a unit in a war zone, Jeff's premonitions had saved the team from ambushes and hidden bombs over and over. He was the real deal. A newly hatched clairvoyant.

His buddy, Rick, had been given the gift of healing. He could put his hands on an open wound and make it disappear. In fact, he'd just done so for Carter, the day before.

They'd all been helping Jeff with a mission of his own less than a week ago, to stop a local woman from being kidnapped. Jeff'd had a vision that showed the woman was in danger, and he'd gone charging in to change the outcome. Carter had been on the support team when a shooter had opened fire in the local mall.

Carter had taken a hit to the thigh and had stayed behind when the team left the scene. The team had taken the female target with them, and they'd tasked Carter to interface with the local authorities and see to the safety of another woman, who'd gotten caught in the middle.

Her name was Hannah Sullivan. A pretty redhead with dazzling blue-gray eyes. She'd been working at the mall, running a kiosk in the center of the wide walking area between the rows of shops. Jeff and his lady had taken shelter there for a few minutes, with Hannah, in the middle of the gunfire. When they'd made a run for it, inviting Hannah to seek safety with them, she'd revealed that she couldn't run. She had a cast on her right foot, and she would only slow them down.

They'd left her behind, but not unprotected. Carter had moved position to stay with Hannah and do his best to keep her safe. He'd already taken the hit in the leg by then, so it was somewhat logical that he be the one to stay behind when the rest of the team made tracks. It wasn't like leaving a guy behind on some foreign battlefield. They were in the States. Not hostile territory.

The shooter had been quickly subdued by local police, and Carter had done his duty, being the point of contact for the authorities, representing the unit. When they had realized he was bleeding, the questions had stopped in favor of medical assistance. He'd kept Hannah with him, and she had submitted to a quick check by the ambulance attendant.

Carter had overheard her talking about her foot, and that she was under care of a surgeon and primary care team at the VA hospital not too far away. When Carter heard that, he'd flashed his military I.D. and asked they be taken to the VA for treatment. Both of them. He hadn't been prepared to let Hannah out of his sight. He'd wanted to know more about her and make sure she would be okay.

The ambulance had taken them to the VA, and he'd submitted to the local doctors' treatment. They'd easily removed the bullet and sewed him up. They'd also taken care of Hannah. Doctors from her care team had come down to the Emergency Room, where Carter and Hannah had been given beds next to each other, separated by only a thin curtain that wasn't closed most of the time.

He'd been able to hear about her foot through the flimsy curtain. Her doctors sounded concerned because, they had said, it wasn't healing properly. Carter didn't like that, but there wasn't much he could do about it. Unless... Rick might be able to help her. But, no. Rick's superpowers were top secret. It would be incredibly difficult to get clearance for Rick to help someone not already in on the unit's secret.

As it was, the doctors had clucked over Hannah, but all agreed that she was no worse for her ordeal in the mall. She'd been discharged, and Carter had wanted to leave, too, but they wouldn't let him. They'd stuffed him in a room after patching him up and told him to stay put.

He'd stuck it out for a few days at the VA. Hannah had surprised him by coming to visit. She'd thanked him again for staying with her during the gunfire and asked if he wanted anything from the little shop in the basement where they stocked candy, snacks and other items. They commiserated about the blandness of hospital food, but eventually she'd had to leave to go to a regularly scheduled appointment with her physical therapist, also located in the same large building, but on another floor in a separate wing.

The following day, his unit commander, Captain Haliwell, had gotten him released from the VA hospital. Carter had returned to the island yesterday, where Rick had done his magic. Carter was good as new today and exercising with his unit. As it should be.

"Heard anything about Hannah?" Jeff asked Carter as they ran along the beach with the other guys.

"I talked to her before I left the hospital. She came to visit me, to see how I was doing." Carter's tone was filled with surprise that she would make a special trip out to see him when he knew how difficult it was for her to get around in that cast.

"How's her foot coming along?"

Carter frowned. "She's been going to the VA for it, but something's wrong with the way it's healing. Did you know she was a vet? She served in Afghanistan and was wounded by a roadside bomb. That's how her foot got messed up in the first place. Her tour was almost up, and after that, she decided to try civilian life again."

"Can't blame her. Especially if the foot isn't healing right," Jeff said as they finished their run. He and the others dropped to the sandy beach to do pushups, Carter beside him. "Maybe Rick could take a look," Jeff added, surprising Carter. He'd wanted Rick to look at Hannah since he'd found out about her problem, but he hadn't really thought it would be possible.

"I wonder if the captain would allow it?" Carter mused, hopeful.

"Only one way to find out. You should ask him. She did see us in action, so it's not like she doesn't know who we are. And she's a vet. Rick's talent is going to waste out here with just us to look after. I bet he'd be happy to help her," Jeff added.

"You're right." Carter felt determined. If Jeff, of all people, suggested he ask, then he would. Sometimes, since gaining his foreseeing gift, Jeff would hint at things that turned out to be very good ideas in the end, without coming out and saying he'd foreseen it all in a vision. "I'll look into it after breakfast."

"Good man," Jeff replied, his tone satisfied. Carter got the distinct impression that he'd been maneuvered by his clairvoyant teammate, but he didn't mind. He'd been wanting to get some help for Hannah, and Jeff's suggestion opened a pathway for him to try.

Carter made a point to seek out the captain once the PT session was over. No time like the present to start the ball rolling.

CHAPTER ONE

Hannah was back at the mall, manning the kiosk a few days after the shooting. Mall traffic was down a little, but Long Islanders were pretty resilient. They'd taken the news story that the mall gunfire had been caused by rival gangs having a turf war with alacrity. Hannah knew it hadn't been any sort of gang action. For one thing, the men who had been the target of the gunfire were military.

Oh, they might not have been wearing actual uniforms, but she recognized what they were. She'd served alongside men like them for a few years, herself. Okay. Maybe not exactly like them, but she'd seen SEAL teams and Green Beret units come through the forward base where she'd been stationed, a few times. The guys from the mall looked like that. Same hard edges, hard bodies and state-of-the-art weaponry.

They hadn't used their firepower in the mall incident. If they had, the whole darn place would've been shot up to hell and back. The only people who had fired at the mall had been the bad guy and the local cops. Thankfully, there had been only one shooter, and the cops had been able to take him down—with a little help from the guy the Spec Ops team had left behind to watch over her.

Carter. That had been his name, he'd said. Whether that was his first name or his last name, she had no idea. It seemed to serve as both.

He was a dreamboat of a guy with chiseled features and the bluest of blue eyes. He'd been injured, too. The gunman had caught Carter in the leg while he'd been moving to cover the petite woman at the center of the knot of big men. She and another guy had taken cover behind Hannah's kiosk for a few minutes. Rose. She'd taken the time to introduce herself just before she and that other man had run for cover farther down the mall.

Hannah hoped Rose and the others had gotten away clean. She didn't really know what had been the cause of all the ruckus, but it was pretty clear it hadn't been gang warfare. At least to her. It had looked more like the shooter was after Rose and those guys were taking her to safety.

Just like Carter had been detailed to see to

Hannah's safety, even though he was injured, himself. He'd stuck by her side until the mayhem was over, and then, he'd even insisted on riding in the same ambulance with her to the hospital.

She hadn't been hurt. Not in that incident, at least, but Carter had insisted that she get checked out. He'd spoken quietly with the local cops and the ambulance attendants, and they'd both been transported to the nearby VA hospital. Only after they'd settled Hannah on a bed in one open ER spot and Carter in the very next bed, with only a thin curtain ineffectively granting them token privacy, had he allowed them to treat his gunshot wound.

She'd heard Special Forces guys were tough, but she hadn't realized how tough until she saw for herself the wound he'd insisted was "nothing" for more than an hour. She'd listened shamelessly as the ER doctor tut-tutted over Carter's injury. The bullet had still been lodged in his leg, so the doctor had wanted to put Carter under general anesthesia while he dug it out, but Carter had adamantly refused.

The doctor hadn't been happy, but had eventually agreed to inject a local anesthetic while he did the job right then and there. Carter didn't make a single sound of pain throughout the procedure, though she had heard the doctor warning Carter that the local anesthetic would only dull the area, not take away sensation completely and that it might still hurt. A lot.

Regardless, Carter didn't groan or suck in his breath. Nothing. Only a mild observation that the bullet wasn't as deep in there as he'd thought. Hannah was shocked. He was *watching* the doctor dig the bullet out of his own leg! Talk about hardcore.

A few minutes later, the doctor had stitched up the wound and left Carter an I.V. drip of very strong antibiotics. Hannah would have observed more, but another doctor had come to her bedside with a bunch of questions.

Hannah had given the emergency room doctor the names of her primary care physician in the VA system and the specialists she'd been seeing upstairs at this very hospital. They had been able to pull up her records on one of the rolling computer stations the nurses used, and they'd called her foot doctor to come down to the ER for a consult. While they waited, the ER doctor looked her over quickly, just to make sure Hannah wasn't hiding any sort of serious injury.

A few minutes later, her usual doctor had peeked around the curtain and after greeting her, asked the usual questions about her level of pain and discomfort. He spent a few minutes examining what he could see of the skin above and below the cast, testing her reflexes and ability to feel different sensations in her toes. Just like he did every time she saw him.

"I kept telling them all that I was okay, but the guy in the next bed insisted I come in," Hannah had explained, once again, this time to her doctor.

"Ah," the doctor had said, her face clouding with a hard-to-read expression. "Well, if you don't have any new injuries, I suspect there's another reason they wanted you to come in. In fact, I have orders not to release you until you've spoken to a Navy commander who's coming in especially to see you."

That had struck Hannah as decidedly odd. She was a sergeant in the Army. She'd had no idea why the Navy would be interested in her. Unless maybe Carter was a Navy SEAL or something. She had listened hard to see if she could learn more about his identity—his rank or any other information—but they'd been very circumspect about discussing any personal information. She decided the staff had probably been given a heads-up prior to the ambulance's arrival, and had known ahead not to speak too much about Carter's records.

One minute, she'd been minding the kiosk for her friend, Lulu. The next, she'd been involved in some sort of classified gunfight in the middle of the local mall, then swept to the hospital when she clearly didn't need to be, taking up space in the Emergency Room. Then, a highly ranked naval officer had arrived.

Commander Lester Kinkaid had been waiting for her in a clearly borrowed office when one of the nurses wheeled her out of the emergency room. The commander had greeted Hannah by rank and name, proving that he'd dug around a bit in her records to learn a bit about her. She wasn't sure what she'd been expecting when she was taken to see the naval officer, but his words had surprised her.

"No doubt, you've figured out that the men

who were in action today at the mall were a military unit," Kinkaid had said without preamble. "For reasons that should be obvious, we don't want that data known to the public. A story is already being circulated to the news media blaming rival gangs for the gunfire," Kinkaid had gone on. "Aside from you, nobody else really saw anything in the mall. Most ducked for cover the moment they heard shots fired. It was just your bad luck to be stuck in the middle of it all." He shook his head. "For us, that's potentially good luck since, based on what I've seen of your record, you're a level-headed sort of soldier who knows how to follow orders."

She hadn't known what to say to that, so she'd remained silent. Always a good option, she'd discovered, when dealing with unknown officers, even if they weren't in your chain of command.

"Sergeant Sullivan, I'd like to know if we can count on your discretion in this matter," Kinkaid had said, meeting her gaze with a fiery expression in his intense eyes.

"Sir, I don't intend to talk to the media, even if they somehow track me down. I recognize the level of skill in the men I saw in action today," she'd told the commander, meeting his gaze frankly. She wasn't scared of this guy. Not exactly. Her career in the military was already in question. If her leg couldn't heal properly, that would be it. Career over. That knowledge gave her a freedom to speak that she otherwise might not have had. "I don't intend to out any

Special Operators. Not today. Not ever. I'm a patriot. I don't understand what they were doing in action on U.S. soil, but it was pretty clear to me that they were defending someone, not causing the problem. In fact, I don't think they even fired a single shot. They were just evacuating at least one person who appeared to need their protection. Who she was or why she needed that kind of guardianship is, frankly, above my pay grade."

Commander Kinkaid had eyed her for a long moment, as if weighing her words, then nodded. "I'm glad you feel that way. And I can tell you that what happened wasn't planned or sanctioned. I'm playing clean-up, and I appreciate your cooperation. I know you're on medical leave and I'm not in your chain of command, but I will write a letter of thanks to go in your file. And please know, you can always call on me for a recommendation, if you ever need one."

He had stood up from behind the borrowed desk that had more than the regulation number of potted plants on it and reached into his pocket. He had given Hannah his business card, on which was printed simply his name, the Navy seal, and a contact number. She'd never seen a card like it, and she had gotten the sense that there was a lot more to this commander than met the eye.

Hannah had been escorted home by VA personnel. They had loaded her into one of the vans they used to transport patients and driven her home. The driver hadn't spoken to her and left her at her door with only a short farewell.

Hannah had gone into her house, using the crutches she'd had with her all along, but hadn't used until then. She'd raided the fridge and fed the cat that came to her back door sometimes. Then, she'd turned on the television and watched the local news report on the mall shooting with very few facts and not much story. They simply reported it and moved on to the child abuse trial that was currently causing a sensation in the local area.

Hannah had gone about her life, as normal. She'd gone back to the VA a couple of days later for her regularly scheduled physical therapy. She'd gone early so she could visit Carter and thank him again for staying with her while all hell had been breaking loose in the mall around them. She had been doing very minor physical therapy even while waiting for the joint to heal, but when she talked to her orthopedist after the therapy session, the news hadn't been as good as she'd hoped.

Lulu had asked Hannah to fill in at the mall again, for the next week or two, while Lulu dealt with some personal issues, and Hannah had agreed. Sitting at the kiosk wasn't her favorite thing to do, but moping around the house was worse. At least at the mall, she talked to people and got her mind off her damned foot for a few minutes at a time.

The good thing about filling in at Lulu's kiosk was that her friend got everything set up ahead of time, and all Hannah had to do was sit there, watch things and take money when someone purchased an item. This sedentary gig was the only kind of job she could do with her foot the way it was. But helping Lulu wasn't really a *job*. It was more just helping a friend.

Technically, Hannah was still in the Army. At least until they took her off active duty permanently because of her injury. She knew she didn't want to stay in if she couldn't rejoin her unit. If they were going to give her a desk job, she might as well get out and try to get on with her life as a civilian. Right now, of course, everything was up in the air until they made a final decision about her stupid foot.

"Hi."

The male voice jerked Hannah out of her reverie. She looked up to find the man who hadn't been far from her thoughts. Carter. His bluer-than-blue eyes gazing down at her, a slightly nervous smile on his firm lips.

"Carter," she said, then felt foolish for not returning his greeting in a more convention way. "I mean, hi. How've you been?" She looked down at his leg. "Should you be walking on that so soon?"

He shrugged off her concern. "I'm fine. Good as new. I just wanted to see how you were holding up," he said, surprising her. "If you get time off for lunch, I'd be happy to take you someplace to get something to eat."

He was inviting her to lunch? The Special Forces hottie who had fueled more than one late-night fantasy was actually here, asking her to share a meal? She could hardly believe it.

"I usually go to the café over there. It's

close, and I can hobble over reasonably quickly and still have time to eat." She smiled at her own misfortune.

"I like their sandwiches," he replied, glancing over at the café and back to her. "If you don't mind the company, it'd be my treat."

"Okay. Thanks. That would be nice."

Nice. Such an insipid word. Of course, she couldn't tell him that her inner voice was doing a cheer at the prospect of spending more time with the mysterious super-soldier. She'd thought she'd never see him again, but she was thrilled to discover she'd been wrong on that score.

"Lulu will be dropping by any minute to cover lunch," Hannah told him.

"Lulu?" he asked.

Hannah pointed to the sign over the kiosk that read *Lulu's Treasures.* "She's a friend. This is her shop. I just look after the kiosk from time to time, since I've been home, when she needs a break."

"I'm glad I caught you, then." He smiled at her, and she almost forgot to breathe. Damn. He had a killer smile.

"I'm sorry I'm running late." Lulu arrived in her usual flurry of activity, not even appearing to notice the big man standing nearby as she opened the locked compartment where they kept their personal items while running the shop. "The good news is, I can stay for the rest of the day, so you're free, Hannah. Thanks for standing in for me this morning." She straightened up and finally seemed to notice

Carter standing there. "Oh, sorry. Can I help you?"

"No, ma'am," Carter said, still grinning. "I'm just here to take Hannah to lunch."

"You are, are you?" Lulu's bubbly personality gave a lot of innuendo to her words, as did the rather obvious look she gave Hannah. "Well, don't let me stand in the way. Go. Have lunch. Enjoy." Lulu handed Hannah her purse from the cupboard and shooed her away.

Hannah would have loved to set her friend straight, but she was already embarrassed enough. Instead, she just put her bag over her shoulder, picked up her crutches and hobbled off, Carter at her side.

Suddenly, Carter understood why Jeeves and his new lady had counselled him to wait until today to check on Hannah. Those two could see the future, and they'd probably had some kind of vision or intuition that Hannah would be free to spend more time with him today. He'd have to remember to thank them for the good advice when he got back to the island later. For now though, he was going to enjoy his lunch—and maybe the rest of the afternoon—with Hannah, if he could convince her to spend it with him.

Something about her had compelled him to find her, again. She'd been so stoic during the action in the mall. Not like he'd expected a woman to react to gunfire. Not at all. Maybe he was a bit of a caveman, but he'd expected hysterics, or at least, some show of fear. Instead, she'd been as calm as any of the guys he worked with on a daily basis. Cool and professional.

He wondered what she'd look like in her uniform... And, for the first time *ever*, the thought of a woman in military garb made him more than a little horny. Maybe it wasn't the uniform, but the woman wearing it. He'd liked to have seen Hannah in action, in the desert. He had wondered if he'd have been as attracted to her if their paths had crossed out there, on duty, and he had come to the conclusion that the answer was definitely yes. *Emphatically* yes. There was just something about Hannah that both impressed the hell out of him and made him want to know her better.

Lunch was a good place to start. Midday meals weren't as threatening as dinner. He could keep it casual and ask lots of questions. Maybe reveal a few non-essential things about himself and learn more about her in the process. At least, that's what he had planned.

They walked over to the café slowly. Hannah was good with the crutches, but he refused to rush her. Every step looked painful, and he wondered again, what he might be able to do to help. He'd talked to the captain about her, and Captain Haliwell had shared a few things about her file without letting Carter see the actual paperwork. That would be a breach of privacy and protocol. But, the captain had mentioned a few highlights of her career that only made Carter want to know more.

When they were seated in a booth with a good view of all the entrances into and out of the dining room, she smiled at him. For a moment, Carter lost his train of thought. Her smile had that effect. It was open and honest…and amused…at him.

"I took a jiu jitsu seminar one time with a highly-ranked sensei who had trained with ninja masters in Japan," she told him. He wondered where she was going with this conversational gambit. "We all went out after the seminar, as a group, to a local sushi place. The sensei picked the table with exactly this sort of vantage point. Even at the meal, he was still teaching. Observe all exits. Never sit with your back to a door. Things like that. You just did the same thing." She chuckled at him, even as she opened her menu and looked at the day's specials.

Carter felt heat in his cheeks and was momentarily stymied by the fact that she'd made him blush. He hadn't blushed since he'd been in high school.

"It's the training," he blurted out after the silence had dragged a bit. "I can't help it."

"Special Forces training, right?" she challenged, levelling her gaze at him as if she already knew the answer to that question.

"Well…" When had he lost control over this situation?

"It's all right. I know you probably can't talk about it. But I've seen your kind of soldier in action before. In the desert," she told him quietly. Her eyes looked lost for a moment before she blinked and came back to the present moment.

"Look…" He tried to regain control. "Suffice to say, we're both in the Army. I heard the VA doctor call you sergeant." He hoped she'd take that opening and move in the directions he wanted to explore.

"I was promoted just before my injury," she told him, nodding.

"When did it happen?" He pitched his voice low, trying to be sensitive in case she didn't like talking about it.

"Two months ago. One minute, I'm in the armored vehicle that's moving along a dirt road. The next, I'm flying through the air."

"Roadside bomb?"

She nodded. "Yeah. I was lucky. It killed the guy who was driving. Corporal Lutz. He was a good kid."

Carter pursed his lips. He knew how she felt. Losing comrades in the field wasn't a great feeling.

"I'm sorry," he told her in a gentle tone. "I've been there, too. I know how hard it sucks."

She blew out a breath, and her gaze rose to meet his, again. "You've got that right." She shook her head and sighed. "But what about your friends. Did everybody make it out of the mall all right? I've been wondering about that woman. She said her name was Rose."

"She's fine. I was the only one hit that day," he admitted with a sheepish expression.

She smiled, and again, he noticed just how lovely she was. Wholesome, yet with hidden depths that made him want to explore.

"If I hadn't seen it with my own eyes, I wouldn't believe you'd been shot only a few days ago," she told him, shaking her head. "I'm glad Rose is okay. If you're still in contact, please tell her I said hello."

"Roger that."

CHAPTER TWO

Hannah liked the way he talked. Soldier speak was part of his natural vocabulary, it seemed. He also didn't treat her like a fragile female. She'd seen respect in his gaze, both during the action at the mall and here, today. Respect and something a lot hotter.

Or maybe, that was just her imagination. Wishful thinking.

No way a drop-dead gorgeous hunk like Carter would be interested in a beat-up NCO like herself. Or...would he?

He had stunning good looks. Chiseled features and brown hair streaked with golden highlights as if he spent a lot of time on the beach, in the sun. His physique was world class. Even loose civilian clothes couldn't hide the breadth of his shoulders or the hard body under the fabric.

And those eyes. The blue of them had haunted her dreams for days after the mall incident. They were penetrating. As if he could see into her soul.

She had suspected the tension of the moments in the mall had made her romanticize his appearance in her memory, but she'd been wrong. He was just as delicious here and now as he had been then. Maybe even more so, now that no bullets were flying and she wasn't a sitting duck for the shooter spraying bullets all over the mall.

"I'm a sergeant, too," he told her out of the blue. She realized she'd probably been staring at him, and the silence had dragged on a bit too long. "Though I've been in grade longer than you have." His smile was charming. Utterly charming and disarming. Damn. "Congratulations on the promotion."

"Thanks."

She was saved from having to make more small talk by the arrival of the waitress. The woman was familiar with Hannah and greeted her like an old friend. They chatted for a few moments as she took their orders, then she left, promising to be right back with their beverages.

"Your friend, Lulu, has some nice pieces at the kiosk. I may come back and pick up one of the Sanskrit inscribed pendants as a gift for our captain's wife. She's sort of the unit mascot at this point. She mother-hens all of us," Carter said, his tone ironic.

"That's sweet. Lulu has a lot of nice gift

items. She tends to focus on emblems or mottos that mean something in different languages. She does a lot of traveling, so she finds suppliers all over the world."

The waitress came back and delivered their drinks, telling them their food would be out in a few minutes. Hannah felt only a little awkward sitting in this place where she usually ate alone. Carter was a handsome devil, but he was also very good at putting her at ease. Now, if she could just stop staring at the man and mooning over his good looks, she'd be all set.

"I liked the look of the bracelet that said *Anuugacchatu Pravaha*, too," he said, when the waitress left.

"It said what?" Did he mean to imply he could *read* Sanskrit?

"It means *go with the flow*. I've always liked that saying," he told her as he stirred his coffee. "I was thinking the pendant that says *Abhay* would be nice for my friend's wife."

"What does that one mean?" And how did he know what they said without reading the little cards on the back of the boxes?

"Literally *fear of none* or *fearless*." He chuckled. "Hal's wife is definitely fearless. She's also kind of small and cute, like a kitten that doesn't know exactly how to use its claws yet, so we've all sort of taken her under our collective wing."

"Do you actually read Sanskrit?" Hannah had to know and asking the blunt question seemed to only way to get the answer, even if it could seem a bit rude. Hopefully, he'd just take it as curiosity.

25

His expression shuttered a bit. "Yeah, well, I'm a language specialist. It's part of what I do in the Army."

"I knew a woman who'd been recruited into Intelligence, and they sent her to learn Russian, though she already spoke Korean," Hannah offered. "That was a few decades ago, though. I expect, nowadays, they want folks who can speak other languages."

"Arabic," he said quietly. "I grew up with a kid who spoke Arabic at home, and I learned a lot from hanging around him and his folks. I branched out from there, and yeah, Sanskrit was a fun challenge."

"Wow." She was impressed. She sensed he was a little ill at ease talking about his language skills, so she didn't press to know more. "That's pretty cool," was all she said. Time for a change of subject. "They were going to send me for some specialized comms training, but with the injury, I'm not sure that'll go ahead now."

"That's a shame."

"Yeah, I was looking forward to broadening my knowledge, but those are the breaks." She shrugged.

"Speaking of breaks, what's the deal with your foot, if you don't mind me asking?"

Wow. She hadn't expected such a direct question, but he'd answered her nosey questions, so she figured it was only fair.

"When the bomb went off, I went flying. I sort of landed on this foot first, I guess, and I broke a lot of bones. They pieced them together as best they could, but it doesn't seem to be healing according to expectations," she told him. It was hard to say it out loud. She'd been told more than once that her injury was life-altering. She just couldn't wrap her head around the idea that she might never walk without assistance again.

"That's rough," Carter said, his tone commiserating. "You know, one of my friends is a doctor. He's got a talent, you might say, for working miracles. Maybe he could take a look, if you want."

"That's nice of you, but I've had five or six different expert opinions, and they all say the same thing. Time. I just have to wait it out and see if it'll heal properly. If it doesn't, they'll take further action, but their options are somewhat limited by the amount of damage that was done." She sighed, hating the prognosis. Something about Carter made her go one step farther, to tell him the whole truth. "Honestly, last week, the doctor in charge of my care told me he's leaning toward marking me down officially as permanently disabled. If that happens, I'm never going back to my unit."

"Is that important to you?" Carter asked softly.

She met his gaze. "I left the job before it was done. That bothers me."

Carter nodded. "I understand."

She felt sure he did. He was just about the only person who seemed to grasp why going back to active duty was important to her. Maybe it had more to do with getting back to normal—whatever that was—or maybe it was her sense of duty. She wasn't sure what it was, but something made her want to make everything go back to the way it had been before her injury.

It might be selfish, but she was honest enough with herself to acknowledge that she wanted her old life back. Pre-injury. When she could walk and run and dance, and think nothing of it.

She knew it probably wasn't going to happen. Not anytime soon, at any rate. Possibly never.

The sooner she came to terms with that, the doctors all said, the better off she'd be, but she just couldn't bring herself to give up hope. There had to be a way. Her body had to listen to her hopes and dreams and get better. Didn't it?

"I really think you should let my buddy take a look at your foot," Carter said, once again, his tone mild, but also insistent. "It couldn't hurt, and you might be surprised. He might be able to help you."

He seemed so hopeful that she found herself agreeing. Plus, it meant she would see Carter again, which suited her just fine. He was easy to talk to, and he lit a fire in her that reminded her that she was female. She might be injured, but she was pleased to discover she could still feel attraction for a hunk of a guy with a killer smile.

"All right," she told him. "You arrange it, and I'll submit to yet another round of prodding and poking at my bum foot." She managed to chuckle wryly. "But I'm not getting my hopes up."

"That's okay," he replied, smiling now in that way that set her insides on fire. "Just as long as you let him take a look, I think you'll be pleased with the results. I'll take care of everything. Are you doing anything tomorrow?"

"Tomorrow? You mean to see you doctor friend?" She was surprised he wanted to do this so soon. Usually, doctors had long wait times to get an appointment. This doctor must be a really good friend.

Carter followed Hannah home, though she didn't see him. He kept a few cars between them, so she wouldn't notice. He just wanted to make sure she got home safely. She'd given him her phone number, so he could set things up for her to see his friend, Rick, tomorrow. What she didn't know was that Carter would be bringing Rick to her home. It was the best way to do this without drawing too much attention.

The unit was based on Plum Island right now, and for the most part, they had to stay on base. There were foreign agents actively seeking to capture any member of their unit, so when they did venture out, they had to be very, very careful about how they proceeded. In fact, Carter wasn't alone. None of the guys were allowed out in public alone.

Right now, Jake and Wil were in another car, following Carter, following Hannah. He knew they were back there, and they were all connected by the tiny tactical radio transmitters they used in the field. They might not be wearing their uniforms off-base, but they were kitted out with as much of the gear as they could manage without drawing too much attention.

For Carter, that meant a handgun in an ankle holster, as well as various knives and other weapons hidden on his person. The radio had gone in his ear as soon as he'd parted with Hannah, and he'd checked in with the guys who'd kept him under close watch while also keeping a lookout for possible trouble. They had his back for this mission, as he'd had theirs countless times in the past. The unit all looked out for each other.

Once Hannah had made her way slowly into her little house, Carter conferred with the other guys. A little discreet surveillance was in order. He'd start by riding around her neighborhood, observing the layout and possible ambush points. Then, tonight after dark, he'd go out on foot and check out her backyard and what he could see of the house itself, from outside. If he was going to bring Rick out here tomorrow, they needed to know as much as possible about the layout and possible threats.

Carter started by the simple act of rolling down his window and listening. He wanted to know what languages other than English, if any, were prevalent in her area. Since his gift had to do with language, he could learn a lot about a place, just by listening. He drove around the area slowly, observing people in their yards or doing chores around their homes. Within an hour, his patience was rewarded by some interesting dialects of Hindi, Bengali and some form of Mandarin, but nobody was talking about anything subversive, much to his relief.

It was a modern, middle-class neighborhood, with the usual children laughing and playing, teens shouting at each other and their parents, older folks sitting on the patio or working in their gardens. A cross-section of cultures and absolutely no hint of anything sinister at all. At least not right at that moment. Which was good. Carter had developed a habit of expecting the worst and being surprised when it didn't happen, but he supposed, after the past few months, he was lucky that was the only problem he had.

He cruised through a drive-thru burger joint and picked up some food. The team in the car behind him did the same. They'd been coordinating their movements all afternoon and would continue to do so until they headed back to the island late tonight. First, though, they'd wait for the sun to go down, so they could do a little more reconnoitering around Hannah's house.

They'd drop a few surveillance cameras that they could access remotely, too. Someone would be watching her place overnight, to make sure it continued to be safe for the visit tentatively scheduled for tomorrow. Carter liked the idea of keeping an eye on Hannah's place. He liked the feeling of trying to keep her safe.

She didn't know him all that well, nor did he

know much about her besides what Captain Haliwell had shared from her personnel file and the small amount she'd shared with him over lunch, but Carter felt a real affinity for the feisty sergeant. She had guts, and she didn't really complain all that much about her medical issues.

That she was gorgeous on the outside was obvious. She had long red hair that she kept back off her oval face. Big blue-gray eyes blinked at him from under curling lashes that were thick and lustrous. She had a wholesome kind of beauty that didn't need a lot of augmentation, though he thought if she'd made even the tiniest effort, she'd knock his socks off.

As it was, he had a hard time keeping himself professional when she smiled at him. That wide, genuine smile that she didn't seem to use much. Probably because of the ordeal she'd been through—and was still going through—with her foot. She had a purity about her that was incredibly appealing and a competence when she needed to act that was very seductive to a man like Carter.

When he'd seen her that first time at the mall, in the middle of an active shooter situation, she'd been calm and sort of resigned to what was going on around her. Frustrated too, with not being able to move quickly out of the path of danger. He'd liked her then, and the attraction had only increased in the time since.

He hoped Captain Haliwell would give the thumbs up to the mission Carter was planning for tomorrow. Ever since they'd gotten back from overseas, they'd had to be careful. They'd been stuck on base for the most part, except for brief forays onto Long Island. They'd fought a few battles, but nowhere near what they were capable of dealing with. For men used to a lot of action in the field, they were going a little stir crazy just sitting around, being examined and tested.

They were used to defeating the enemy and helping people. They'd fulfilled that mission all over the world. It felt frustrating to not be able to do that here, on their own home soil. Helping Hannah would be a step in the right direction. Carter knew Rick couldn't wave his magic hands and heal her completely in one go. He *could*, but that would likely raise too many questions. Still, Rick might be able to start a process that would lead to a more complete recovery for Hannah. That would be the best outcome, but Rick had to see her in person to do his own examination first.

Which was why getting him to her was so vital. They had to do it safely for all concerned. The unit couldn't draw attention to itself when they knew there were foreign agents actively seeking them out for capture. It seemed the leaders of a few different countries in the area where they'd acquired their new gifts, wanted them back.

None of the guys really understood how the enemy thought capturing the members of the unit would cause them to work for the opposition. Maybe they had some weird beliefs about taking away the powers that had been gifted to the team by that old man in the ancient city of Babylon. Carter didn't know—though he would love to find out what they thought would happen if they ever succeeded in capturing even one of the Green Berets of his unit. Carter suspected the bad guys would have a very rude awakening, indeed.

CHAPTER THREE

Overnight surveillance—done remotely via cameras and sensors Carter and the guys had placed around Hannah's property—showed no activity, so Captain Haliwell gave the go ahead for the mission the next day. Carter was thrilled, though he did his best to contain his enthusiasm as he loaded up with the other guys on the boat that would take them to a private dock near Hannah's hometown that had been secured for their use.

They had several landing options all along the coast of Long Island, which allowed them to cross over from the tiny island on which they were stationed to just about any area of the much bigger island off the coast of New York, at almost any time. They had water supremacy in the area due to all sorts of sensors placed on buoys surrounding the island. They also had nature itself, helping out, in the form of dolphins.

They really were highly intelligent creatures. Some of the guys in the unit could sort of speak to higher-level animals now, but only Carter could truly understand their language. On the rare occasions he'd been around dolphins who were making vocalizations, his new ability to understand every language ever spoken had kicked in, somehow, to let him understand what the dolphins were saying to each other.

It had freaked him out. He'd tried it since with other animals, but most didn't have the higher brain functions that allowed for true language. He was able to get single words from time to time, but not complex sentences. The guys had teased him, calling him Doctor Doolittle for a while, but thankfully, they'd dropped that particular nickname when his ability didn't really produce results with other animals.

He was a linguist. He understood languages. If the beings didn't have a true language, his new skills weren't really activated. That's the conclusion he'd come to with the help of the specialists that had been flown in to evaluate the entire unit.

Most of the keepers were gone, for now, off to report directly to brass in Washington about the strange happenings with their unit. It was just as well. Everyone was sick of being monitored and tested. They seemed to have leveled off, for the time being, and they were slowly gaining mastery over their new abilities.

Carter was glad to have time out from under the microscope. He and the other guys were getting antsy, being stuck on the island, and a little time off gave them opportunity to do things for themselves. His mission to help Hannah was one of those things Carter had pushed for the group to take on ever since their paths had crossed during the mall shooting.

Luckily, Jeeves and his new lady, Rose, were in agreement. They'd met Hannah first, when they'd taken cover behind her kiosk, with her, during the shooting incident. When they'd made a run for it, Hannah'd had to stay behind because of her bum foot, and that was when Carter had been detailed to keep an eye on her. He'd already been shot, so staying behind made sense, but the moment he met Hannah, he'd felt an attraction that only deepened the more he was around her.

Carter was driving Rick in one vehicle. Jeeves was driving the car behind them with Jake. They were just about to pull up to Hannah's house when Jeeves pulled over unexpectedly. Carter saw it in his rearview mirror, so he pulled over, as well.

"What's up?" Rick asked, looking behind them.

"Jeeves stopped," Carter said, watching the other vehicle in his mirrors.

"Guys? Jeeves is doing his trance thing," came Jake's voice over the tactical radios they all had in their ears. "Stand by."

Carter waited impatiently to hear what the

newly-clairvoyant member of their unit might have to say. When Jeeves finally spoke over the radio, the news wasn't exactly what Carter wanted to hear.

"Hannah's place is bugged," Jeeves said quietly. "Inside. Cameras and audio. She doesn't know. Someone put her under high surveillance a short while ago. Probably right after the mall incident," Jeeves reported. "And there's one troubling image I saw of Hannah installing at least one of the cameras herself."

"Damn," Jake said, accompanying his thoughts with a low whistle over the radio.

"We can't go in," Rick said unnecessarily.

"And we should probably remove our cameras and sensors from the yard before anyone else notices them," Jeeves put in.

Carter saw the wisdom in the suggestion, but he just couldn't get over the idea that Hannah had put up cameras in her own house to catch him out. There had to be some other explanation.

"This is your op, Carter," Rick reminded him.

Rick was an officer, but Carter knew they were all off the clock, doing this on their own time. He wasn't going to pull rank because he knew this mission was important to Carter, personally.

"I think we'd better get to the bottom of this. Either there's some innocent explanation for your vision of her bugging her own home, Jeeves, or she's on the wrong side of all this. Either way, we need to know. If she's innocent, we need to protect her. If not..." it pained Carter to say it, "...we might be able to use her to get to the enemy."

"Call her," Jeeves advised quietly. "Tell her to come out of the house. That you're taking her to the doctor."

"That could work," Carter agreed. "But where do we take her?"

"Back to base," Rick said. "We don't really have any other choice."

"Hal's not going to like it," Carter mused, but knew he had few options. "Okay. Rick, get in the chase car. Maybe you could draw straws and the loser calls the captain to give him a heads up? I'll call Hannah while you're repositioning."

Rick got out of Carter's vehicle and jogged back to get in with Jeeves and Jake while Carter dialed Hannah's number. She picked up on the third ring.

"My doctor friend has an opening this morning. Do you still want to see him?" Carter asked after they'd exchanged greetings.

"Sure, I guess so," Hannah replied, not sounding entirely enthusiastic. "What time?"

"I can pick you up in about fifteen minutes, if that's not too soon for you, and take you there," Carter offered.

"Um. Okay. I guess that could work. Thanks. I'll see you in a bit."

She didn't sound like a traitor, Carter mused to himself as he ended the call after saying goodbye. There had to be an innocent reason for her to put surveillance in her own house.

Maybe she was putting in a security system or something. But most people aimed the cameras around the property, not in the actual house. There had to be more to what Jeeves had seen. Had to.

Hannah was excited to see Carter again. She knew she should curb her enthusiasm. Nothing would probably ever come of anything between them. She had little doubt that he was on a very different life path than she was. Her injury had sort of stopped her in her tracks, and she didn't know how things were going to work out with that, much less how it might impact any romantic liaisons.

When her doorbell rang, she was ready. She made her way to the door on her crutches and opened it to find him on the other side.

"Are you ready to go?" he asked after exchanging greetings.

"All set," she told him. She locked the front door behind herself and followed him down the front walk to his car.

It was a different vehicle today from the staid sedan he'd driven yesterday. This was a four-wheel-drive utility vehicle, similar to ones she'd driven in the Army. It was higher off the ground than a regular car, which made it a little easier to get her bad leg inside, though she needed a bit of help getting up high enough to get her butt on the seat. Carter was courteous, helping her into the vehicle and putting her crutches in the back. He also made sure she was buckled into her seatbelt before he started the car.

"Nice Jeep," she said, meaning it. The dark green vehicle was a civilian model, but it wasn't all that much different from the military version she had gotten used to overseas.

"Thanks," Carter replied easily, pulling into traffic. "I thought it would be a little easier on your foot." That was so thoughtful of him. She was really touched. "It also has some other great features, as you probably know. This one has a permit to drive on certain beaches."

"It's a dune buggy?" She knew some people got bigger tires and special permits to be able to off-road their vehicles on certain beaches where such activities were allowed. She'd just never seen one up close.

"Somewhat," Carter admitted. "It's got the larger all-terrain tires and some suspension modifications. It's a lot of fun on the sand."

"I'll bet." She had enjoyed driving the Army vehicles over rough terrain overseas. It was a powerful feeling to know you could drive over most things that would give a regular car pause. "I can hear the hum of the tires on the concrete," she observed as they rolled down one of the North-South highways, heading toward the waters of the Atlantic Ocean.

"Yeah, they have big treads," he told her conversationally. "The noise is a trade-off for the utility, but it's not too bad, right?"

"No, not bad," she agreed, though the faster he went, the louder it became inside the cab of the vehicle. She let the conversation die down as he concentrated on driving and that humming sound filled of the passenger cabin.

When he didn't take any of the exits, but kept heading south, she started taking note of where they were. They were getting awfully close to the shore, and traffic on the highway was down to just two lanes.

"Where are we going?" She realized she should have asked that question before ever leaving her home, but it was too late now.

Panic wanted to rise, but she tamped it down. Panic wouldn't help her in this situation. If Carter was intent on kidnapping her or accosting her in some way, she wasn't really in a position to oppose him. He was too big and strong, with undoubtedly lethal skills. She might've at least fought back before her injury, but as things were, she didn't really stand much of a chance against him.

Carter looked at her, his expression pained. "I really am taking you to see my friend, the doctor, but we're going to have to do it a little…unconventionally."

"Why?" she demanded. At least he wasn't looking at her as if she was his next meal. That had to count for something, right?

"Because your house was bugged," he said, flat out, sounding angry. As if he had a right to be upset about the fact that she had a security system in her home. "I was going to bring him to you, but not with cameras all over the place."

"First of all…" She tried really hard to keep her calm and put her thoughts in order. "There are only three security cameras inside the house on my new system. I installed them myself.

There's one in the living room, pointed toward the front door. One by the back door, and one in the basement." She ticked them off on her fingers. "Second, how the *hell* do you even know about them?" She glared at him. Better to be righteously angry than scared, she figured.

"I know because it's my business to know these things and not bring my friends into danger," he replied, as if that was any kind of real answer. She puffed out her breath and rolled her eyes at him. "And there are way more than three cameras inside your home. There are audio pickups, too."

"I repeat: How the hell do you know that? And are you serious? I only put up the three measly cameras that came with the alarm system. There were no audio pickups. Nothing else besides the sensors for the doors and windows and a motion sensor I had Lulu put in the upstairs hall for me. She also put the camera in the basement, since I can't really do stairs right now."

He kept driving steadily, taking them all the way to the end of the highway and off onto side roads. He pulled into one of the many beach entrances—this one looking private, rather than public. He didn't stop in the lot but went right onto the sand, shifting the vehicle easily into four-wheel drive.

Sand flew, and she reached for the handhold above her door while the vehicle rocked on its off-road suspension. She could see the water now, and he was heading straight for it. Was he going to stop? Or turn? Or something!

Then, she saw it.

"You're kidding, right?" She blinked, but it was still there. Off to the right was a military landing craft, sitting, waiting, with its ramp down.

"Hold on." He turned the vehicle and lined up with the ramp, taking it at a higher speed than she thought safe.

He bounced off the sand and onto the treads of the ramp, then onto the wide deck of the landing craft. Holy crap. She'd been abducted by the military. No way did civilians have these kinds of craft. This was a military op, and somehow, she was right in the middle of it. Again. Like she had been in the mall.

Or, perhaps, this was all *because* of the mall incident. Yeah, that made more sense. She'd seen through the men in civilian clothing for what they really were, and though she'd agreed not to say anything about them, somehow, she was still under surveillance by them. *Much* closer surveillance than she'd thought possible, considering they seemed to know the contents of her house. She didn't see how they'd know about her cameras—and the alleged others— unless they'd had someone actually break into her home and take a look around.

Damn.

This was just getting too complicated for her. She was only a sergeant. A run-of-the-mill infantryman. She didn't mix with Green Berets. She'd never, in her life, been on an assault craft like this one, but she recognized it, even as men appeared on deck and secured the ramp in its upright position. Someone in the wheelhouse got the thing moving, and before she knew it, they were underway, heading out into the Atlantic.

"Where are you taking me?" She turned an accusatory gaze on Carter. He didn't like that look, but he supposed he deserved it.

"Just getting you away from any possible surveillance for a little chat." Carter tried to sound nonchalant. Friendly, even.

"This is all because I recognized what you were at the mall?" she asked.

"That and the surveillance in your home. We need to nail down which side you're on."

"*Which side I'm on?*" Outrage filled her tone, and she looked ready to spit nails as she turned her head to stare out the window, silently fuming.

Carter found it almost amusing, though he would never let her know. The more he was around Hannah, the more he felt in his bones that she was on the right side of things. There was no way she was working with the enemy. No. Way.

He'd stake his life on it.

But... He wouldn't risk Rick or any of the other guys on his own gut feelings. In order to get her the help she needed for her foot, she needed to prove herself trustworthy to the rest of the unit. Only then, would she be brought into the circle. There was really no other way to have Rick do his thing without bringing her into their confidence—at least a little.

Carter still wasn't sure how they were going to pass off Rick's abilities. They'd discussed strategy on that, but Rick wouldn't know for certain how to proceed until he examined her in person. The current hope was that she could see him a few times over a period of weeks, and he could zap her with his healing vibes—or whatever it was—a little bit at a time, over a longer period, so the healing wouldn't seem quite so miraculous. Rick had never really done that before, but he thought it might be possible. Again, he'd made no promises until after he had a chance to examine Hannah's foot in person.

"I am not a traitor," Hannah said in a low, almost deadly voice.

Carter looked over to meet her gaze. Indignant fire burned in her eyes.

"I'm inclined to believe you," he told her honestly. "But I hope you'll understand that the other guys, who haven't interacted with you, have their doubts. I can't put any member of my unit at risk, even if I, personally, think you're on the level."

"Small comfort after you've already abducted me and are taking me God knows where." She harrumphed and looked away again.

"We're going to an island just off the coast of Long Island. Not too far away, actually. I can have you back home in time for dinner, if things work out," he told her.

"If your friends decide I'm not working for the enemy, you mean." Yeah, she was pissed. Her words were sharply cut off, as if with a knife.

"Yeah, that. And if Rick gives you the all clear on your foot."

"Rick is the doctor you mentioned?" She seemed interested, despite her anger.

"Yes, ma'am."

"And he's a member of your unit?" She scowled. "What can a Special Forces medic do for my foot that a specialist can't?"

"Rick's an M.D., not a medic, though he serves that purpose when we're in the field," Carter admitted.

"What kind of Special Forces unit has its own doctor?" She turned to look at him again, the anger in her expression tinged with curiosity.

"We're a very specialized unit," Carter replied, unable to hide his grin.

"A linguist, I sort of understand," she told him. "But a doctor?" She shook her head. "I don't really get that at all. Doctors aren't special operators. They stay behind the lines, out of combat, if at all possible."

"Not this one," Carter said, cocking his head to the side. "Our unit is a bit different from most others. We're all specialists of one kind or another. We were brought together because of our unique abilities, and they've only sharpened since the formation of our unit. We go in to both fight and investigate. To get to the bottom of what's going on in a particular area, using all our skills." He couldn't say much more than that without saying too much, so he left it there.

The landing craft was well on its way to the

island on which there was a highly classified military base. Bringing Hannah there was a concession. They needed to ask her questions, but none of his unit was really safe off-base at the moment. They were being hunted, and though it wasn't ideal to bring more people to the secure facility, they'd made an exception for Hannah.

She'd already seen them in action once, though she hadn't seen much, really. Just a bunch of big guys escorting a woman out of the mall under fire. They hadn't showcased any of their unique abilities, but her military experience had led her to draw her own conclusions—correct conclusions—about what kind of unit they were. Though, there was no way for her to know exactly how special they were. Not yet. Probably, not ever.

CHAPTER FOUR

Hannah did her best not to freak out at the unexpected turn of events. Whatever she'd gotten herself into here, it had the stink of being something sanctioned by the government. No way were these guys so well equipped without government backing, nor could they operate with impunity on and around the island, as they had been doing, if some sort of officialdom didn't know and approve of their existence and actions.

She'd been in the Army long enough to know that elite military units like this didn't take a crap on U.S. soil without forms filled out in triplicate and commanding officers' heads on the line. The military wasn't sanctioned to operate on U.S. soil, except under very special circumstances. The fact that these guys were keeping such a low profile, yet operating heavy equipment and even participating in shoot-outs, was troubling. Though, she had to admit, the unit hadn't fired a single shot during the mall escapade. They'd taken all the fire from the enemy without returning any.

It had been the local police first responders who had shot back and stopped the shooter in the mall, while the military guys had quietly and rapidly gotten the hell out of Dodge. With a civilian in tow. It had certainly looked to Hannah that the woman, who'd introduced herself as Rose when they were all hiding behind Lulu's kiosk, had been the one the guys were protecting—and extracting from the danger zone.

For some reason, Hannah's home security system—and whatever else they claimed was in her house—had set them off. Everything had been fine, and she'd really believed Carter was being honest with her about getting his friend to look at her leg...for whatever good that would do. But, now, they had basically abducted her, and she had a feeling she was in for a lot of tough questioning when they got where they were going.

Fine. They could ask her over and over, but the answers wouldn't change. She was secure in her innocence of whatever they were thinking. She wasn't the bad guy here. She would just wait it out until they got their heads out of their asses and figured that out.

The landing vehicle slowed as it approached a small island, and she took a deep breath. The ordeal—whatever it was going to be—was about to start. The landing craft lowered its massive ramp, and Carter started the Jeep and drove it off, onto the island, without a word. He drove off the beach and onto a paved road. She noted the official-looking buildings all over the place, as well as the men and women in uniform, who watched silently as the vehicle passed.

The uniforms were right. She was definitely on a military base of some sort, though she hadn't realized there was one out this far. It was definitely isolated. A perfect place for top-secret goings on. *Damn.* Hannah was both relieved and concerned. Relieved because her Army record should mean something to these people, and concerned because they seemed to look at her as a potential enemy at the moment.

She was one of the good guys. She just had to convince these people of that.

They didn't speak as Carter parked the vehicle just in front of a large building some distance from the beach. He pulled up close to the door, for which she was grateful. She was good on the crutches as long as the ground was level, but the great outdoors was a challenge if there was sand or gravel. There were both present in the small parking lot, as well as grass and dirt around the edges.

"This is our stop," Carter said as he got out of the Jeep and came around to her side to help. He got her crutches out of the back and handed them to her without comment.

He was different now than he had been with

her before. Did he really believe she could be working for the enemy...whoever that was? She wanted to shake her head and scoff at him, but she knew the situation was serious. Still, she was completely innocent, so truth was her ally. They'd see how wrong they were, and then, Carter would have to apologize. Whether or not she'd accept his apology remained to be seen.

"For what it's worth..." Carter spoke quietly as they paused on the way to the building. "I believe you. I don't really think you're playing for the other side." He gave her a soft smile that went a long way toward melting the ice that had formed around her heart. "The other guys just need to be sure. Humor them, and then, we can get on with this."

"Simple as that?" She let some of the irony sound in her voice. "I'm not accustomed to being thought of as some kind of treacherous double agent."

Carter shook his head. "No, ma'am. I imagine you aren't." He sobered a bit and met her gaze squarely. "But remember, I don't think you're one of the bad guys."

"Well." She began hobbling along on her crutches toward the door again. "That's something, at least."

She didn't want him to know exactly how grateful she was to hear his vote of confidence. She was scared. Deep down, she was afraid of everything that had happened in such a short time. First, the gunfight in the mall—a place she had always thought safe. That had shaken her, and she'd had nightmares for the next few nights. Nightmares she hadn't had since she'd come back from overseas. The sound of gunfire had brought it all back, and suddenly, she was in the desert again, danger all around.

Then, just as she'd come to terms with all that again, Carter shows up and abducts her. She'd gone from mild hope for a new doctor's opinion on her foot to being swept up under suspicion of being an enemy and transported to some secret military base for questioning. She was thrown off balance by the events of the day, to be sure. But that's probably what they wanted. She knew the techniques, though she'd never had to use them. Get an enemy prisoner—keep them off balance for questioning. She hated to think that the rest of Carter's friends might think of her as the enemy.

They were met at the door by a man she'd seen only in passing in the mall. She'd pegged him, at the time, as the unit commander, and she was somewhat pleased to have her suspicions confirmed.

"Sergeant Sullivan," he said, his voice neither friendly nor threatening. "I'm Captain Haliwell. If you'll come this way."

This way led to a room just off the main hallway that looked like some sort of living room or rec room area. There was a ping pong table set up in one corner, as well as a couple of lumpy-looking couches set around a large screen. Low tables were clear of clutter, but she could easily see them holding pizza or beer or whatever snacks the occasion required when the unit was off duty.

She supposed she should be grateful to have been led to a rec room rather than a holding cell or interrogation room. She sat at the small table to one side of the door, where the captain indicated. He wasn't in uniform, and neither was she, so this wasn't *official*, in that sense, but she knew they were all very aware of the fact that she was under some sort of suspicion. She didn't like that. Not one bit.

"Thank you for coming here today, and I'm sorry it had to be such an unusual trip. We hadn't planned on it, but when our men discovered transmitters in your house this morning, Plan A went out the window, and we had to improvise."

"How did you discover these alleged transmitters? Did you have people infiltrate my home?"

She didn't give a damn about rank or protocol at the moment. Her blood was up, and she was angry enough to ask what she most wanted to know. This captain wasn't in her chain of command. She'd never even met him before. She didn't owe him anything, even if it was potentially foolhardy to disrespect a superior officer.

"No, Sergeant. We have other ways to discover such information. Your house wasn't invaded by us." Clear in his words was the idea that somebody else had broken into her home and placed bugs and cameras and who knew what else.

"I already told Carter that I'd put in the

security system. I put sensors and cameras facing into a few of the rooms since my disability, so I would be able to monitor the upstairs and the entrances and exits without having to get up." She didn't like this at all, but so far, the captain wasn't accusing her of anything. Maybe this wouldn't be as bad as she'd feared.

Haliwell nodded. "A wise precaution. I'd have probably done the same in your situation. The thing is..." He paused and narrowed his gaze on her. She tensed, sensing a change in his mood. "The thing is, the frequency that system is working on is separate and apart from the other frequencies transmitting both audio and video out of your house. You admit to putting in the commercially available system. But, if you put in that one, you also had the ability to put in some of the military-grade hardware that's currently transmitting from inside your house."

She had to take a breath at his assumption, then logic prevailed. "That's if you assume I had access to such things. I have never been involved with surveillance technology. I bought an off-the-shelf system for my home when I got laid up. That's the extent of my so-called ability."

"So you say," Haliwell insisted.

She sensed he was going to say a whole lot more when the door to the room opened, and a clearly civilian woman in a pink T-shirt came in. She looked upset. Sort of like a mini-tornado about to let loose. Hannah recognized her as she walked farther into the room. It was Rose. The woman who'd been shot at in the mall and taken to safety by this military unit.

"Oh, for heaven's sake." Rose stomped in, her sneakered feet not making that much noise and somewhat lessening the effect. "Hal, Hannah is not a traitor."

"I know you're new to all this, Rose," the man she'd called Hal replied, a long-suffering look on his face, "but we have to check things out. You know what's at stake here."

"*Pfft.*" Rose made a shooing motion with one hand. Hannah might be willing to talk back to the captain, but she would never presume to scoff in his face. Rose had some brass ones, that was for sure. "She's no danger to you," Rose went on, seemingly unaware of the captain's growing annoyance. "In fact, she's more like you guys than you realize. She's a warrior. A survivor." Rose sent Hannah an encouraging smile. "She's here to help. Trust me. And, if you don't trust me, ask Jeff."

Hannah found herself looking over her shoulder towards the doorway, where the man she'd seen with Rose in the mall was leaning against the doorjamb. He looked amused more than worried about what his girlfriend was getting into with his superior officer.

"Is this true, Jeeves?" Haliwell asked the man in the doorway.

Jeff—or Jeeves, as Haliwell called him—straightened from his leaning position and moved into the room. "Sorry, Cap'n. I'm afraid Rosie is correct."

The man's accent was British, but he was part of this strange specialist unit? Hannah just wanted to shake her head at whatever it was she'd gotten into with this group. They weren't like any military unit she'd ever seen—or even heard of—before.

"I believe Miss Sullivan poses no danger to us," Jeff went on. "However, the danger to her has increased. She is most definitely under surveillance by our enemies and probably has been ever since the mall incident."

The captain sighed loudly. "I was hoping we wouldn't have to bring any more civilians into this."

"With all due respect, Hal," Rose spoke up, "Hannah is not a civilian."

Hal shook his head. "Technically, you're right, but she's not one of us."

"She needs to be," Rose insisted, standing up to the growly captain.

For her part, Hannah was both insulted and fascinated. She, a sergeant in the Army and veteran of a war zone, wasn't *one of them*, but Rose—the most civilian a civilian could be in her pink T-shirt and sneakers—was? This group just got more and more bizarre.

"You've seen something?" Hal asked Rose and Jeff, both.

Jeff nodded, his expression solemn. Rose followed suit, oddly not saying anything, though she'd been very talkative up to this point. Something was very strange about these people, and Hannah wasn't exactly sure she wanted to know what it was.

Hal sat back in his chair and sighed. "Well, if you've seen it, you've seen it. We might as well bring Rick in and get on with the original plan for the day—getting her foot examined and fixed up."

"That's it?" Hannah asked, surprised by the sudden change in tone from the previously-menacing captain. "What are you? Some kind of intelligence specialist?" she asked Rose directly.

Rose chuckled. "No, I'm a fortune teller. In fact, I've met your friend, Lulu, a few times, at the shop where I used to work. She came in to pick up some stock that she'd bought in partnership with the shop's owner. Nice woman."

"Wait. You work in a new age store?" Hannah found this hard to take in.

Rose shrugged. "I did, up until the mall shooting. I was Madam Pythia, one of the fortune tellers working out of the Sacred Way Psychic Shop," she said, smiling. "I work here now, as a civilian contractor."

That didn't really explain much, as far as Hannah was concerned. What could a self-described fortune teller do for Uncle Sam as a civilian contractor? It seemed farfetched. Rose had to have some other qualification to put her in that position, but she was obviously not going to talk about it, so Hannah didn't push. She was just glad Rose had somehow been able to call off the dogs. Haliwell still looked a little grumpy and Hannah wasn't going to test that by asking him anything directly.

The man called Jeff had left the room

momentarily but returned now, with another man in tow. The other man smiled at her and came right over, placing a large bag on the table. This was the doctor, then. The bag was his medical kit. Hannah looked around in confusion as Haliwell got up, and the doctor moved chairs around so he could sit next to her.

"I'm Rick," the new man said, still smiling as Haliwell moved to stand next to Jeff and Rose, a short distance away. Carter stood with them, watching all with no comment. "I've seen your file from the VA," Rick began, "but I have to do my own evaluation, if you don't mind."

Hannah's head was spinning. These folks had turned on a dime—all on the say-so of Rose and Jeff. Hannah wanted to know what those two could possibly know about her that would make the commanding officer back off so fast and so completely.

She turned the chair so she faced the doctor. He'd placed himself facing her. "Carter, can you roll that over here?" he asked while he opened his bag. He didn't take out any of the equipment in it, but it was standing ready, in case he needed anything.

Carter brought over a rolling stool that was just the right height to prop up her foot so the doctor could examine it more easily. After he helped Rick position the stool and her foot on top of it, he didn't go far. He stood behind her shoulder, out of the way, but ready should she need his help.

It was so tempting to lean on Carter's

presence. To accept the comfort he offered just by standing there. But, even though she still found him to be the most compelling man she'd ever met, she was really confused by the events of the day, so far.

His unit was just...odd. Really, really odd. There had to be more to this than met the eye, but she hadn't a clue what it was. Not yet. Possibly, she wouldn't ever know what this strange group was all about. She was off balance. Things had happened really fast. Strange things. Confusing things. Upsetting things.

All she really wanted was some time alone to process everything, but that was not meant to be. Rick took off the protective bootie she'd been given at the VA on her last visit, and the sock beneath. Her foot looked like something out of Frankenstein's lab. It was puffed up and bruised many different colors. It also had a jagged scar and the remainder of surgical staples that had closed the incisions made while they'd tried to put her foot back together.

Rick put his hand over the joint, lightly touching, and closed his eyes. Hannah wondered what the heck he was doing. Didn't he need to see it to figure out what was wrong? Shouldn't he be looking at the x-rays? The scan reports? Instead, he was just touching her ankle with his eyes closed. In a day of weird events, this shouldn't have surprised her, but when his hand started to give off heat that she could feel—really feel—in her ankle, she freaked out completely.

"What's he doing?" she asked, nervous. "That's hot," she complained, shocked and scared at something she didn't understand. She would have pulled her foot away, but Rick's hands clamped down on her ankle, and Carter's hand covered her shoulder.

"It's okay," Carter told her in a low voice. "Trust me. This is good."

"Good?" She looked up at him over her shoulder. "My ankle is on fire!"

"Yeah, that's a side-effect of his process," Hal piped up from where he stood with the others. "If you feel that, it means he can definitely do something for you."

"What *is* this?" Hannah looked at all of them, wanting to understand and failing utterly.

Then, the fire really took hold, and she couldn't think of much else besides her foot and the searing pain of whatever it was Rick was doing. She couldn't see what was going on with his hands in the way and a particularly searing pain had her clenching everything, including scrunching her eyes shut.

She'd been a fool to trust these people. Rick wasn't helping. This hurt as bad as it had when it happened!

"Son of a..." Hannah was vaguely aware that she was cursing, but she didn't care.

Whatever the so-called doctor was doing, it hurt like hell, and she wasn't shy about using every cuss word she'd ever heard and aiming them at the people who had kidnapped her, interrogated her like some common criminal and were now torturing her under the false pretense of helping her.

"Impressive vocabulary," someone muttered, sounding oddly complimentary. She let it wash over her. All she could really think about were the nuclear explosions happening in the nerves of her foot.

After a particularly wrenching pain, she heard something fall to the floor. A group of somethings, she decided, hearing repeated little tinkling clatters, but the relief that followed made it hard for her to concentrate.

"They certainly used enough hardware." Haliwell's voice came to her out of the fog of pain and relief. Carter grunted in reply and squeezed her hand. When had he taken her hand? Hannah couldn't recall. "What happened to the slow approach, doc?"

"Sorry, Captain. Couldn't do it, after all. Not with all that stuff in there. It had to come out, and there's no way to hide it." The doctor didn't really sound all that sorry.

"It's okay, guys. This is the way it's supposed to be," Rose put in, her voice calm and collected. Their words came to Hannah through a haze of intense discomfort, but it was starting to ease a bit.

CHAPTER FIVE

Hannah opened her eyes to look down at her ankle and saw a small array of shiny screws and other bits of metal she couldn't easily identify on the floor, all around the stool on which her leg still rested. It didn't make sense. Then, she focused more closely on her leg. The discoloration was… It was gone.

"What the heck?" she whispered. "What did you do?" Her gaze flew to the doctor. He was frowning, his focus still on her foot.

"Just give me a moment more to get rid of the rest of the swelling," he said through clenched teeth. She took a good look at him and realized he looked paler than he had. Almost sickly, but determined, his teeth set in a near-grimace. It was as if whatever he was doing came out of his own personal energy.

She wanted to pull away, but Carter squeezed her shoulder, drawing her attention. "Let the man finish," he urged.

This, she realized, was why he'd been so insistent that she see his friend, the doctor. Rick had some kind of…amazing ability…a gift, if such things existed. And, after experiencing what she was experiencing right now, she had to believe it did, in fact, exist. Rick was a healer, like something out of a fairytale. He was healing her with his touch.

She could feel the pain leave her. The pain that hadn't quit since the day she'd been injured. It was gone. And her ankle looked almost normal. As she watched, the final traces of swelling went away as if by magic.

"Now, that's just weird," she muttered, watching the latest round of bruising fade from her skin. She looked up at Rick as he removed his hands from her ankle and leaned back as if he'd just run a marathon. "What *are* you?"

"These days?" Rick sighed tiredly. "I'm not even sure of the answer to that myself."

Captain Haliwell reached down and began picking up the various bits of hardware off the floor. When he had it all, he straightened and placed the small pile on the table next to Hannah.

"No way to hide this, I guess," Haliwell said.

Hannah just stared at the pile of bits. "Did all that come out of my ankle?" Her throat was so dry she could barely get the words out.

"Your surgeons did a good job, but that stuff was never going to hold your bones together in a way that would actually work," Rick said. He definitely looked tired. Drained. Whatever he'd done had taken a lot out of him.

"What did you *do*?" she asked, unable to articulate all the questions competing for space in her mind.

"Try to move it," Rick said in response, the amused curl of his lip daring her to give it a whirl. He shifted his gaze from her face to her foot and just watched.

Feeling as if she was in a dream, she moved her foot slightly. It didn't hurt. For the first time in ages, it didn't hurt! She tried another small movement. And another. She rotated the ankle gently, then pointed and flexed her foot. This *was* a dream. Had to be.

"No way," she whispered, even as she kept moving her foot in ways it hadn't moved since her injury.

Tears sprang to her eyes that she didn't bother to hold back. It was a miracle. An honest-to-goodness miracle.

She looked up at the doctor, tears streaming down her face, her eyes wide. "I don't know what you are, or how you did that, but I..." She paused to catch her breath. "I can't thank you enough. There are no words..."

"Don't thank me yet. Let's see you stand on it," Rick said, brushing her words aside as if embarrassed.

Standing? Seriously? He wanted her to stand on her shattered ankle?

She hadn't stood—really stood—on her own two feet in months.

65

Hannah lowered her foot off the stool. It didn't hurt when it made contact with the floor. Hope rose higher in her heart. She'd pretty much resigned herself to never running again. Or dancing. Or doing much of anything that required two reasonably working ankles.

Rick stayed seated opposite her, as if he didn't have the energy to stand, but also watching her foot carefully. Everybody else seemed to hold their breaths. Carter was right behind her, ready, she had no doubt, to catch her should she fall. He was that kind of guy.

Gingerly, she put weight on her feet and then pushed to a standing position. Nothing hurt.

Sweet Lord, nothing hurt!

Hannah stood on both feet, then tried just the injured foot. It held her weight easily, though her leg muscles felt weird from not being used in this way for a while. Not painful. Just a little weird at first.

She stood. Then, she walked. Heck, she felt like turning cartwheels!

"It feels fine," she said, a bit breathless from the awe that filled her at these developments. "Like nothing ever happened. Like the last few months were just a bad dream. A nightmare from which I've suddenly woken up."

Yeah, she was crying. She didn't care. These were happy tears. Nothing to be ashamed of.

Rick stood, still watching her progress as she turned to face him again. She walked right up to him.

"I have little doubt you outrank me, but can

I hug you, sir?" she asked, unable to keep the tears out of her voice.

Rick smiled, looked a little surprised, but opened his arms. "Sure. Why not?" He let her hug him and then stepped back with a little red flush on his cheekbones, though he bore it well. "A hug is more than I get from these guys, even after I save their miserable lives."

"If I'd known you were so easy to please, Rick, I wouldn't have bought you that case of scotch," Hal put in, clearly amused at the doctor's expense.

"Or the Army-Navy game tickets," Carter added.

That's when Hannah realized that this amazing doctor had been healing the guys in his unit. "You're why Carter isn't still on crutches after having a bullet taken out of his leg," she blurted the thought as it came to her. "I thought his wound was worse when we were in the hospital, but then he shows up walking as if he'd never been shot."

Rick nodded a bit sheepishly. "Guilty as charged, I'm afraid. There's not much else for me to do around here, now that we're sidelined," he said. "When I see something that needs fixing, I fix it."

"Like you fixed me," she thought aloud again, wonder in her voice.

"Sergeant," Hal broke into her awestruck silence. "Why don't you join us in the mess? We can discuss this over coffee."

Shaking her head, Hannah followed the captain out of the room and down the hall. The others peeled off, going their separate ways, but Carter remained by her side. She'd wanted to thank Rick again, in case they hustled her away now that she'd been seen and treated, but he slipped away down a side corridor before she could speak.

When they reached the mess hall, which was really just a large room with a cafeteria-style serving area on one side, opposite a bank of windows that looked out onto the beach, Carter led her to one of the tables. Hannah had marveled the entire way about her foot, which seemed good as new, as if nothing had ever happened to it. There wasn't the slightest twinge of pain from the joint. Some of her muscles weren't used to moving normally anymore, and they would require strengthening, but that was nothing. Not when she could walk again.

The mess hall was empty, but a coffee urn stood ready, hot go-juice in the half-full pot. Hal walked directly to the coffee urn and started dispensing black java into three cups. He handed the first to Hannah, and she took it gratefully, moving to get some creamer and a dash of sugar for hers from the supplies to the left of the urn. Carter got the next cup, leaving it black as he waited for her. Once Hal had his own cup, he led the way to a table in the far corner of the large, empty room.

She could just hear faint bumps and clangs from the kitchen area. Staff in the kitchen on the other side of the buffet line were probably preparing the next meal. The corner Hal chose for their conversation would give them privacy. There was no way the kitchen staff would be able to overhear what they talked about unless they started shouting, and she certainly didn't plan on any of that.

She was too grateful to these men. This unit...and their incredible doctor.

"The first thing you need to know, Sergeant Sullivan," Hal said once they'd all sat down, "is that nothing you see here can ever be repeated to anyone else. This is all top secret at the highest levels. I wasn't comfortable bringing you in on this, but Carter—and some others in our group—felt you deserved a chance after the mall incident. You were cool under pressure during the shooting, and it impressed the guys who saw you in action. The fact that you were already injured, and that we might be able to do something to help, weighed heavily on our minds. We had more than one discussion about your situation before I gave Carter the go-ahead to contact you."

"I didn't realize that, sir," she said when Haliwell paused long enough that she thought perhaps he was waiting for her to say something.

Haliwell nodded. "I didn't expect you would," he replied. "But the fact remains that, while we all felt it was important to see if Doc could help you, there are farther-reaching issues that must be considered. Secrecy being the main one."

"Yes, sir. I understand," she assured him. "I won't tell anyone what happened here just now.

Frankly, nobody would believe me." She couldn't help the smile that curved her lips as she imagined how that might go down. Yeah, better to not say anything, rather than end up in a padded room.

"The danger isn't only to yourself, Sergeant. Partially because of what you just saw, we've become hunted by agents of at least one foreign government. That's who you saw shooting in the mall the other day," Haliwell admitted.

"Yeah, I knew it wasn't gang-related, but I didn't say anything. The Navy commander who came to see me in the hospital impressed me with the need to keep my mouth shut, and I figured there were good reasons for covering it up. I confess, I didn't really think it could be enemy action on U.S. soil." She was appalled that foreign agents had opened fire in the mall. That wasn't gang warfare. That was terrorism.

Hannah realized why they wouldn't use the T word. Long Island was particularly sensitive to terrorism after the attacks on New York City, which was only a few miles away. Many people on Long Island worked in Manhattan and commuted there every day.

"It isn't a full-scale war, but I'm sorry to say, it's definitely enemy action, and that's not the first time we've had to deal with it since coming back Stateside," Haliwell told her.

Hannah began to understand how much danger followed this unit's steps. Whatever they'd done in foreign lands, it had come back to haunt them. She didn't understand it fully, and perhaps, it wasn't necessary that she should. She'd received her miracle. She was thankful for that and willing to respect the need for secrecy about Rick's amazing ability. That was only fair.

"You have my word of honor that I will never reveal what happened here today," she told the captain, hoping he would hear the truth in her voice.

"Thank you, Sergeant Sullivan. I'm working with base command to get your paperwork updated so that detailed records of your foot injury won't be in the VA system after today. It's best if you don't go back there anytime soon, because there's really no way to explain your current condition to those who'd been treating you before. Also, I'm afraid you're going to have to keep up a little bit of the fiction of having a sore ankle for a while, in public. Ease off the crutches and maybe use a cane for a bit. Pretend to favor the ankle as if it's healing," Haliwell suggested.

Hannah saw the sense in what he was saying. "I can do that. No problem, sir."

"Good." Haliwell slammed back the rest of his coffee and stood but waved for Hannah to remain seated. "Now, the paperwork and computer updates will take a while. I'd like you to stay here for tonight, and we'll return you to your home tomorrow. My wife, Casey, and Rose, of course, can help you settle in. We have some spare clothing in stock for female personnel, and they can fix you up with whatever you need."

Hannah barely had the chance to thank him

before the captain was out the door, leaving her with Carter. It was only mid-afternoon, and so much had happened in such a short time. She was having a hard time taking it all in.

"Do you want to take a walk on the beach?" Carter asked as he finished his coffee. "Give your new ankle a spin?"

"That sounds good," she admitted. She hadn't been able to keep from moving her ankle under the table, aware in one giddy corner of her mind that it didn't hurt anymore.

She finished her coffee and followed Carter's lead in placing the used mug in the bin that would presumably be collected by kitchen staff for cleaning at some point. Then, she walked with him out the door and toward the nearby beach, still amazed with every step that she could, in fact, walk unassisted for the first time in months.

They went slow. Carter didn't speak, giving her time to pick a safe path onto the fringe of sand that met the ocean not too far away. He was looking out at the water, seeming in a pensive mood. Finally, after a few minutes of strolling along, he spoke.

"I'm really glad Rick was able to help you," he said quietly.

"Me, too. And thank you for insisting I see him. I sense you probably had to jump through a lot of hoops to make this happen," she said, feeling grateful.

"Not as many as you might think. Fate might've brought you to the unit's attention during the mall incident, but lately, some of us have come to be big believers in it. Your actions at the mall—your courage and steadfastness—impressed a lot of people. Not just me," he told her.

He'd been impressed by her during that first meeting? The thought surprised her. She'd been the one who was impressed by him and the rest of his friends.

She looked out at the ocean. The view from here was incredible.

"You know, I grew up on Long Island, but I didn't live near the beach. I could get used to these ocean views all too easily," she said, hoping to get the conversation onto safer grounds, just for a little while. There was so much jumbled in her mind right now, it was good to focus on something normal, like the view.

"Yeah, it is one of the nicer spots I've been stationed," Carter agreed. "I'm originally from Portland, Oregon. We have river views there. Not ocean. And it rains a lot."

"I visited Portland once," she replied. "One of my college friends moved there. It rained the whole week I was there, and I was semi-convinced that Mount Hood was a model they set up for tourist post cards, since I never saw it in person from the city. We drove up to Multnomah Falls one day. Pretty place."

"Yes, it is. And yeah, Portland can be very overcast and cloudy, but when the sun shines, it's a great city," he said, a bit of nostalgia in his tone. "Still, I like what I've seen of Long Island. Lots of people in a small amount of space, but every amenity you could ask for, close at hand. Lots of airports, too. And lots of sunshine compared to home, though not as bad as the desert."

"Oh, yeah. That desert sun was brutal," she agreed. "I liked the adventure of going, but I was glad to come back. Though, I would have preferred to do my full tour rather than come back injured."

And they were back to what had happened to her, just like that...and what had happened today, to erase the last months of angst and pain.

"How's the foot?" Carter asked.

"Good as new," she said. "I can't believe I'm saying that. I honestly thought I'd never have full use of it again." She felt tears threatening again, as she spoke but was successful in holding them back this time. "I can't thank you enough."

Carter shook his head. "No need to thank me. Rick did all the work. He's been pretty amazing since he started being able to heal us like that."

"It came on suddenly?" she asked before she thought better of it. "I'm sorry, I know I don't need to know. I'm just curious."

"Don't worry." Carter shrugged as they walked slowly along the beach. "I'd be curious in your shoes, too. Now that you know what he can do, I don't see any real harm in telling you a little more about it." He didn't look at her as they walked along. "Rick was a doctor when he became part of the unit. Like I mentioned before, we're a group of specialists sent in to do more in-depth investigation than most other units are capable of accomplishing. His task, among other things, was to assess any potential bioweapons we might come up against or discover in the course of our missions. He was kind of a germ warfare expert, though I guess since this...change...happened, that's kind of taken a backseat."

"It happened in the desert?" she asked in a low voice, not wanting to pry but really intrigued by both the unit and whatever had happened to make the doctor suddenly able to heal with a touch.

"Yeah, we were ahead of everyone else, as usual. Scouting. We came out of a dust storm to find an ancient city in front of us. Empty, but intact. It was the weirdest thing," Carter told her. "We investigated, of course. There was this tower. We climbed inside and went up and up to the top room of the tower that had a view of the entire city. There was a man there. A man wearing loud colors, like something out of a book. His jewelry was gold, and he had a turban on his head. He was just sitting there, cross-legged, on a prayer rug. Like he was waiting for us."

"Only one man in the whole city? Were they all hiding?" she asked, breathless, but not from the walk.

"Nobody hiding that we could see. It was just empty. Except for the turbaned man," Carter told her. "He talked to us for a while. He was stand-offish at the beginning, but became friendlier as he got to know us. He asked a lot of questions about the world and the state of his country and those around it. He didn't know what the United States was at first, but he caught on. We talked for a long time and then, he said a few more words and sent us on our way. It was the weirdest thing. Normally, we would try to control any interaction with locals. We control the conversation and the timing. We don't answer questions, for the most part— we ask them. But all bets were off with this guy. We didn't stick to mission from the moment the dust storm cleared and we found ourselves in that city. It was like we were under a spell or something."

"Maybe you were," Hannah whispered, not quite sure why she was whispering.

CHAPTER SIX

"You believe in that kind of thing?" Carter asked, turning to meet her gaze.

"I've seen some strange stuff in my life," she answered, not wanting him to think she was either gullible or crazy. "Today was an eye opener, in fact," she reminded him of her most recent brush with the mystical and inexplicable.

"I suppose so," he said, still eyeing her as if he would ask more, but he let it go. She sensed the topic wasn't completely closed, but they were done with it for now, at least. "Well, we left the tower, and after some more exploring, we went back to base. Shortly after that encounter, Hal was hit by a sniper and would have died, but Rick came running and did his thing for the first time. To say we were all shocked would be an enormous understatement. After that, they hustled us home, because it became clear that some of the locals knew or maybe guessed what we'd encountered in the desert and didn't want to let us leave their part of the world alive. They kept gunning for us, and they've kept trying to get us here, as well. That was what happened at the mall. And, we believe, that's who added the *extra* surveillance in your home."

"They bugged me, hoping I'd lead them to you?" she asked. "Seems a bit far-fetched."

"I think they're getting desperate. They knew you had interacted with some of us during the mall incident. There was no way to hide your involvement, since the kiosk, and the fact that you sometimes run it for your friend are both well-known," he reasoned. "I think bugging your house was a precaution on the off-chance that one of us would extend the contact."

"Which you did," she said, putting the final piece of that particular puzzle into place. "So maybe, it wasn't that far-fetched for them to bug my place, after all." She frowned. "I still don't like it. Some stranger was in my personal space, putting in cameras and mics to watch and listen in on my personal life. Nope. Don't like that at all."

"And, unfortunately, you can't remove any of it without blowing the fact that you now know about them."

She growled. "This just gets better and better."

"And, when you get home, you're going to have to act the part of still being injured some more, because they'll be watching." He reminded her.

They walked past some boulders and Carter paused. "Want to sit for a moment?"

"Sure," she replied, moving toward the boulders and picking a likely spot to sit.

Carter settled beside her. They were facing out toward the water, watching the waves.

"I come here sometimes, to think," he confessed quietly.

"I can see why," she said softly. "This is a good spot for contemplation."

"I'm sorry you got mixed up in all this. I know it won't be fun for you to have to hide the fact that your ankle is better, but I really need you to play it cool. Both for our sakes, and for your own," Carter said, turning to meet her gaze. "I hate that you've come under observation by our enemies. If I could rip out all the surveillance and shove it down their throats, I would, but as things stand..."

"Don't worry," she told him, covering his hand with hers. "I understand. I don't have to like it, but I understand."

The moment lengthened and then stretched ever so slightly as some unseen force drew them closer together. Like magnets, they moved slowly toward each other until his lips touched hers, and time stood still.

Even the waves ceased their incessant shushing over the sand while they kissed. Or so it seemed.

This kiss was unlike any other she had ever experienced. It was familiar...somehow. As if they'd known each other intimately before but hadn't been together in a long time. It was impossible. She would have remembered a man like Carter in her life—not that there had been that many to start with.

She'd never kissed him before. Never met him before that moment in the mall. But somehow, he was familiar. Easy. Comfortable. And compelling.

She moved closer, sliding into his arms as if she belonged there. The kiss deepened and stirred things in her she'd thought long-buried. She hadn't been in a serious relationship in a long time. Her career had come first—especially after being sent overseas. It had just been easier to not have anyone waiting for her at home. Her folks were gone. She didn't have much close family. Lulu was really the only person in her life who'd been keeping in touch with Hannah while she'd been away. It was enough.

But Carter made her feel things. Emotional things. Things that made her start thinking about the potential for a relationship with him.

It was impossible, of course. He was in the middle of some sort of top-secret situation, and his unit was being hunted on top of that. It would be ridiculous to try to start a relationship under the circumstances, but her body clearly had other ideas.

She responded to Carter instantly. There was no uncertainty. No hesitancy in her when he kissed her. It was the most natural thing in the world to kiss him back and seek more of his heat, his strength, his hard body.

He drew back, and she didn't understand at first. She tried to follow, but his hands gripped her arms above the elbow and held her back.

"I'm sorry," he said, confusing her even more. Hadn't he enjoyed it as much as she had? He'd certainly seemed to enjoy kissing her if the bulge in his pants was anything to go by. "I shouldn't have done that," he went on, splashing verbal cold water all over her burning desire. The yearning in her body petered out, to be replaced by embarrassment. She tried to retreat, but he didn't let go of her arms. "I shouldn't have taken advantage of the moment," he clarified. "I've wanted to kiss you for a long time, but that doesn't mean I should."

Stymied by his words, she spoke her mind. "Why not?"

"Because I'm in a tough spot, right now. I don't know how this is all going to end with the unit and the foreign agents gunning for us. I don't want to drag you into the mess that is my life, any farther than you already are. It's not fair to you to put you in such danger, and it kills me that those bastards have already invaded your privacy, just on the chance that I'd make contact with you again." He pulled her close and placed a gentle kiss on her forehead. "I'm so sorry, Hannah."

"Don't be sorry," she whispered, unable to say anything else.

She moved away from him, and this time, he let her go. She stood from the boulder where

BIANCA D'ARC

they'd been sitting and walked a short distance away, toward the lapping waves of the ocean.

"Will I ever see you again, after I leave this island?" she asked, not daring to turn around and look at him. She needed to know the truth, and she had a sad feeling inside that she already knew what he would say.

"No. Not if all goes as planned," he told her. She thought she heard regret in his voice, but maybe that was just her own wishful thinking. "I wish it could be different, but it's safest for you if you forget all about everything you've seen here."

She turned to face him and was touched by the pained expression on his face. "I can't forget this," she whispered. Then, she smiled and lifted her foot off the ground, showcasing her healed ankle. "And I certainly can't ever forget this."

Carter shook his head ruefully and joined her in a slight grin. "Yeah, I guess that would be hard to do."

She was saved from making further conversation by the appearance of a platoon of men jogging down the beach from the other side of the base. These weren't the men of Carter's unit. No, these were other men from another command. They were led by the commander she'd seen in the hospital. Navy guys. Each one built like a brute, with sleek muscles and chiseled features.

If her head hadn't already been turned by Carter, she would have appreciated the physiques on display as they made their way in a fast jog past her and Carter. They were wearing only swim shorts, and they were wet and sandy. And holy bulging biceps, Batman. Each and every one of them—including the commander, who was an older fellow—was rock solid with a six- or eight-pack abdomen and tight buttocks. The wet swim shorts left little to the imagination.

"Eyes front, Sergeant," Carter growled in her ear, clearly amused by her reaction. She jumped a bit and had to chuckle.

"Hey, you can't blame a gal for looking," she quipped, startled when a few of the men in the running formation laughed. A couple looked back and her and winked. Even the commander sent her a wave and a grin as they ran past. "Is that a SEAL team or something?" she asked as they began walking back toward the barracks building in the distance.

"Or something," Carter agreed noncommittally. "We're not encouraged to ask too much about the others who are stationed here. We're sort of the interlopers. This is a Navy base, but the brass needed a place to stash us when we got back, and this was the most convenient place, apparently."

"That commander came to see me in the hospital. Read me the riot act about keeping my mouth shut," she observed as they walked. "He's pretty fit for an older fellow," she couldn't help but observe.

Carter just shook his head. "You should probably keep anything you observed pertaining to him and his people under your hat as well, when you get back home. Like I said, we were told not to ask too many questions. This whole place is very hush-hush."

"Understood." She sighed. There was going to be a lot she would never be able to talk about when she went back to her regular life.

This whole adventure was like something out of a dream. Her foot was healed, and she could walk without pain. She would have to fake that for a while until she could reasonably have been healed from a lesser wound. It would be a bit of a drag, but well worth the miracle that she had received.

Her heart was heavy with the notion that she'd never see Carter again. He'd kissed like a dream. Like they'd always been meant to meet...and kiss...and perhaps a whole lot more. Only, they weren't going to get the chance.

Fate was a bitch, sometimes.

Carter was subdued as he walked Hannah back to the barracks. She'd fit in his arms like she'd always been meant to be there. Something about the two of them together just clicked.

He hadn't expected to meet a woman like her—a woman who could change his outlook on relationships and forever. Yet, he had met her. At the worst possible time in his life.

He kept up a façade of civility all through dinner, letting his friends entertain Hannah while he remained a mostly silent observer. The women took to her quickly. Rose seemed like she'd always known Hannah, and they certainly hit it off like old friends. Casey was slower to warm up to Hannah, but she did, too.

He realized Hannah would fit in with these people, if he dared bring her even more fully into his world. It was a big risk, though. For one thing, if he asked her to stay, she'd have to give up her normal life for who-knew-how-long. It would be way too dangerous for her if it was known that she was involved with him. Like Rose and Casey, Hannah would become even more of a target than she was already, for their enemies.

He couldn't do that to her. No way. It was bad enough someone had already broken into her home and placed cameras within. He'd disrupted her life enough.

He wouldn't let it go any further. He didn't want to ruin her life. Oh, he'd make sure she was safe. Once she returned to her home, he'd watch over her. He wouldn't let any harm come to her, if he could help it, but he also wouldn't see her. Wouldn't let her get any more involved with him than she already was. He just had to let her go… For now. Maybe, he consoled himself, sometime in the future, when things had settled down for them all, he'd look her up and see if she was still interested.

Yeah, he could do that. When the time was right and he wouldn't be putting her in danger.

If that miraculous time ever happened.

It was much later that night when Carter heard the click of his door opening. He was instantly alert. He hadn't been asleep. How could he sleep when he knew Hannah was just a few doors down the hall?

But she wasn't a few doors down anymore. No. She was here. In his room. He saw her tempting outline in the faint light from the hallway a moment before she slipped into his room and closed the door behind her with a soft click.

Hannah knew she was taking a chance. She had consciously decided to throw all propriety out the window and seek out Carter in his bedroom. She'd made note of the location of his room earlier, when he'd said goodnight and left her. She'd followed him into the dormitory hallway on the pretext of using the ladies' room that was located on that same corridor and noted which door was his before he went in and shut it tight behind himself.

She knew she might be rejected, but she had to try. She had this one night out of time. This one fascinating span of hours on this special island. She was going to take full advantage of it, even though pouncing on near-strangers in their bedrooms wasn't behavior she normally engaged in. Far from it.

"Hannah?" Carter's voice came to her out of the dark.

She followed the sound of his voice to his bed, finding him sitting up, watching her. She could see him better as her eyes adjusted to the dim light coming in the window. It was a dark, cloudless night, but the moon was up and was giving off faint illumination.

His chest was bare, and the sheet had dipped

low. She wasn't sure if he was wearing anything beneath the covers, and her imagination fired. Would he welcome her into his bed? Or would he turn her away? Only one way to find out.

"What are you doing here?" His voice was deep but quiet in the stillness of the dark room.

"Isn't it obvious?" she asked, moving a step closer, so she could sit on the side of his bed.

"You have to leave tomorrow, no matter what," he told her, his eyes searching hers.

"That's why," she told him. "I want to know. Before this dream ends. I want to be with you."

"Hannah…" His tone deepened. "You don't owe me anything for what Rick did."

She shook her head. "That's not it. Carter, I really like you." She more than *liked* him. She knew she could easily love the man, but she couldn't say that. Not on so short an acquaintance. Especially not when he had every intention of ending their relationship with finality once she was home again.

"But this can't go anywhere," he reminded her.

"Does it have to?" She tried really hard to sound nonchalant. Just a girl, out for a good time, with no thought of the future or of the broken heart she was going to find at the end of this road.

Hannah had already thought about that. She figured the pain she would feel from missing him would be less if she at least had the memory of what it was like to be with him. The not knowing would drive her crazy if he sent her away now.

Carter sat up more, so he could get closer. "I don't want to hurt you," he whispered, and she sensed his capitulation with a bit of triumph.

"I know that," she whispered back as his face neared hers. "I don't want to be hurt, but at this point, not being with you tonight would hurt more, I think. This is my time out of time. My stolen moment. I want to share it with you."

That did it. His lips touched hers, and words were forgotten. Time and space ceased to exist. There was just the two of them. Together.

His kiss was just as devastating as it had been on the beach. Fires ignited in her body, her soul. He took her mouth with an edge of desperation. He seemed to be feeling the same rough desire she was experiencing. As if they were on the same page of a very naughty, very exciting book.

She crawled over him, onto his bed, as he kicked the covers away. She was glad of the full-sized bed he had in his room. She'd been half afraid he would have a much smaller bed, but she'd have found a way to make do with it. She'd have jumped his bones on the floor, if she'd had to. Being with him was quickly becoming an imperative in her blood.

He was wearing only boxers under the covers, she was pleased to find. His body was every bit as muscular and fit as the men she'd been shamelessly ogling on the beach earlier. She was more than a bit out of shape since her injury, but Carter didn't seem to find any fault with her appearance, though she wasn't happy with her own state of fitness, at the moment. She would have a chance to remedy that, now, thanks to Rick and Carter and the chance this unit had given her to reclaim her life.

But it wasn't thankfulness that had driven her to seek out Carter's bed. No, it was need. A need which only escalated as he touched her, kissed her.

His hands were under her tank top, stretching the fabric and seeking her bare skin. She helped him lift the tank top over her head and chucked it to the floor by the side of the bed. She was bare under it, and Carter wasted no time, cupping her breasts and learning their shape.

Her skin cried out for his touch, loving the gentleness in his caresses and the slight trembling of his fingers as he traced them over her body. She leaned into his touch as their kisses resumed. He was both gentle and strong, leading her places she'd never been to before. None of her prior experiences—not that there had been all that many—had prepared her for the exquisite combination of power and tenderness that was Carter's lovemaking.

He was so in control. She felt tempted to see how far she could push him to make him lose that careful control. She wanted to see him wild with desire, if such a thing was possible.

Hannah's fingers went to the waistband of his boxers. With a cunning grin, she tugged them down, over his lean hips, and away. His cock sprang free of the confining fabric, and he was as hard as she'd hoped. Excited. Ready.

Daring greatly, she took him in hand and moved to lick him. She heard the stifled groan that told her she was on the right track, and rejoiced in the feeling of power it gave her to know she had him at her mercy for this small moment out of time. She wouldn't abuse the power. No, she was all for trading the honor back and forth with him. Right now, she would show him a thing or two and look forward to when he took control back from her and did the same—a true partnership in passion.

She licked him then took him deep in her mouth. The growl that came from his chest was exciting.

He let her play for a few moments, but then, he turned the tables on her. He simply lifted her and reversed their positions so that he was on top. He licked his way down her throat and then over her breasts, pausing to pay homage to each excited point. But he didn't stop there. He worked his way down her torso, his big fingers going under the waistband of her sweat pants, tugging and pulling on the fabric until she lifted her hips to help.

The pants and panties beneath came off in one long slide and were deposited on the floor with the rest of the discarded clothing. When he kept kissing his way down her body, her breath caught. Was he going to...?

Oh, yes. He *was*. His talented tongue licked over her clit, making flutters of excitement course down her spine. And, when he gave her the most intimate kiss of all, he drove her absolutely wild with need. A climax hit her, rolling over her like a rogue wave of the most delicious kind. She went with it, allowing it to pull her under, but Carter was there, holding her throughout, her lifeline in a tumultuous world of need and desire.

Dimly, she heard the bedside drawer open and the crinkle of plastic. In one foggy corner of her mind, she realized he was protecting them. Carter was such a good, kind and thoughtful man.

He was smiling when she met his gaze. He rose over her and wordlessly joined them together, even before her climax had fully dissipated. There was a method to the madness, she soon discovered, as another wave built upon the one before. He rode her, watching her reactions and seeming to gauge her desire. Carter played her body like a fine instrument, altering his tempo as her passions rose in concert with his desires.

He plunged into her as the tension rose, and she felt her body respond to his more aggressive motion with answering need. She was with him as he took her over the edge, into the sweetest oblivion she'd ever known. He followed, going with her all the way, taking them to the brink of sanity...and beyond.

CHAPTER SEVEN

Hannah was gone when Carter woke the next morning. Only the disarray of his bed was left as evidence of their passionate time together. He wasn't sure how he was going to let her go, but he knew he had to do so. It wouldn't be fair to her to ask her to live under these conditions. To put her life in danger, just so he could be selfish and have her all to himself. That would be asking just too much.

He showered and dressed in his workout gear with a heavy heart. He'd have to let her go today. There was no use putting it off. The longer she stayed away from her home, the more suspicious the enemy would become. One night, she could probably explain away easily. Any more, and they'd have to come up with some viable reason for her absence and create evidence of whatever backstory they devised. It would get complicated, and the more complicated, the more likely it was for something to go wrong.

Carter didn't talk to anyone as he assembled on the beach at dawn with the rest of the guys. He wasn't in the mood to chat. He just wanted to get this mandatory exercise period over with—something he usually looked forward to each morning—then find Hannah and bask in her presence while he still could.

"Mind if I join you guys?"

Carter whirled around, and there she was. Hannah. In the flesh. Smiling at him...and the other guys.

She was dressed in shorts and a T-shirt, with athletic socks and sneakers on her feet. The ladies had kitted her out for Physical Training. Damn. She looked good.

"Not at all, Sergeant," Hal answered for the group. "Just keep up as best you can."

Carter recognized the gleam in her eye, even if Hal didn't realize he'd just issued a challenge with his casual words. Hannah wasn't a quitter. She would keep up with them or damn near kill herself trying. Carter resolved at that moment to stay next to her and try to keep her from re-injuring herself in an effort to prove something to Hal and the rest of the unit.

He moved next to her as the group moved off in a lazy jog. They were all just waking up. The pace would increase as the session progressed, but they usually started off a bit slower—especially now that they were back

Stateside. He fell into step beside her, and they kept to the back of the line of joggers for the moment.

"Good morning," he told her, uncertain where to begin. He'd missed seeing her in his bed earlier, and that was an unaccustomed feeling for a single guy like himself.

"Morning," she replied. He couldn't tell what she was thinking from her tone. Was she mad at him? Happy? Sleepy? Annoyed? Pleased? He had no clue.

"How's the foot feeling?" he ventured. He was looking for clues as to her mood but decided to tread carefully.

"That's what I'm about to find out. So far, so good," she told him as they loped along at an easy pace.

Ah. So, that's why she was up at the crack of dawn. She wanted more data on how good her ankle was now.

"Guess you won't be able to exercise like this at home for a while," he said, thinking of the surveillance on her home with a frown.

"Even if I still have to play the cripple for a bit, it'll be easier on me mentally if I know for sure how good or bad my ankle and overall fitness is at this point. I'm used to a certain level of performance, and I used to keep to a somewhat strict regimen of exercise. Everything's been different since my injury, of course," she told him.

He thought about that for a moment. He hadn't realized she'd been an athlete. "Do you think you'll change anything now that you've been through this experience?" he asked finally, curious about the way she thought and viewed the world.

She shot him a look, her eyes narrowed. "To be brutally honest, I used to be very much a *no pain, no gain* kinda gal. I think this experience has taught me to be a little nicer to my body. I'll still work out, I'm sure, but I probably won't do the things I hated doing. Life is too short to torture yourself every day, you know? But I like running. I was competitive in track and field in school."

"Oh, yeah?" He felt an imp of mischief take hold of him. "Want to show these bozos how it's done?"

Hannah grinned back at him. "Most definitely!"

They put on the speed and easily outpaced the rest of the guys. The unit cheered Hannah on, shouting compliments on her *footwork*. Doc even jokingly took part of the credit for her return to running.

They got to the rock where the unit usually turned around well ahead of everybody else. Carter signaled a halt and was glad to see that Hannah was breathing hard but not completely winded. She really was in amazing shape, which he would have realized if he'd been looking closely. As it was, he'd been trying *not* to notice every little thing about her because he knew she'd be gone soon, and he didn't want to get any more attached than he already was. Plus, her foot had been the big distraction to this point. Now that she could move freely again, and her foot wasn't such a big deal, he was able to see the rest of her more clearly.

She was beautiful. Not just in a surface way, but down deep, where it counted. On the surface, she was trim and muscular. Lithe and able to keep up with him, which was different. Most women he'd known had been soft and pampered, and they cried if they broke a nail. Hannah had short, well-kept fingernails that wouldn't interfere with her ability to do things. No polish. No nonsense. He liked that.

He sure was going to miss her when she left. Damn.

"They're almost here." Her voice broke into his thoughts. "Do we go back, now?"

"Sure. Why not?" He started off in an easy jog, and she fell into step beside him. They soon passed the rest of the group, still heading in the other direction, and teasing remarks were passed back and forth until they were out of earshot. "We usually do this run then calisthenics on the beach by the barracks before heading in for quick showers, then chow," he told her.

"Good routine," she replied. He looked down at her, and she was watching the beach for footing but also looking off toward the ocean when she had a chance. "Sure is a pretty place to work out. The sand is packed nicely for running, down here near the water line. I've lived on Long Island my whole life, but I've never run on the beach before. I'm going to have to change that, now that I can."

"Not too soon, but yeah, it's great running

down here at dawn," he agreed. "I get up before the rest of the guys and just do a loop around the circumference of the island on my own sometimes."

"Nice." She didn't say anything else as they continued running, the peace stretching between them.

It was easy for him to imagine doing this for the rest of his life. Having her at his side, a partner in every sense of the word. But that could never be. Not with the change he had undergone in the desert and the subsequent target that had been painted squarely on his back. He couldn't subject sweet Hannah to the danger in his life. No more than he already had.

They sprinted the last few yards to the beach behind the barracks then stopped, walking it off for a few moments. Carter could see the rest of the guys loping along, heading toward them, but they still had a few minutes alone. He felt like he should say something, but for once, words failed him. He had to try anyway.

"Hannah, I feel I should thank you for last night. I would have, if you'd been there when I woke up. I'm just sorry—"

"Don't be sorry." She cut off his words. "Don't ever be sorry. I'm not. I wanted my magical day to extend, and you gave that to me," she said, blowing him away. "The only possible regret is that it can't continue."

Did she mean what he thought she meant? Probably not. She was talking about magic, not a relationship. She wanted more miracles and rainbows. He wasn't that sort of guy. He couldn't do fairytales, even if he felt, sometimes, like he was living in the middle of one. Only, his brand of fairytale was darker. More Brothers Grimm than Hans Christian Andersen or Little Bo Peep.

"It can't." He opted for truth, agreeing with her. "I'm glad you see that. Though, you're right. I do regret that."

He couldn't make a move on her with the guys getting closer with each passing moment. Carter wanted to reach out and touch her cheek, draw her close and kiss her like there was no tomorrow, but he couldn't. Just like he couldn't let their relationship—such as it was—go on any longer.

"I'll never regret our time together," she told him. "Just that it had to end."

And then, there was no more time. The rest of the unit intruded on their stolen moments alone, and their private conversation was at an end.

It was that way for the rest of the morning calisthenics and right through breakfast. Other people were around them at every moment, and Carter and Hannah didn't have any further opportunities for private discussion. Carter was glad he'd spoken when he had, but he wished he'd been able to fully express what he was thinking. For a linguist who could speak and understand any language, he was woefully without words when it came time to say the important things to Hannah.

Then, she was leaving, with no more time to

say the things he might want to say, if only he'd found a way to do so. Jeff and Rose took her back to her home, the clairvoyant pair insisting they had to be the ones to drive Hannah. After all, Jeff was the best offensive driver in the group. If they ran into trouble, there was no one better suited to driving them out of it than him.

Plus, he could see the future. He and his lady both had that gift and could take care of themselves. If they said they had to be the ones to drive Hannah home, nobody in the unit was likely to argue with them. Even if Carter had been craving those few extra minutes with Hannah, which he was now to be denied.

Hannah left the island with mixed feelings. She was surprised when Rose and Jeff declared they would be the ones to see her safely home. She'd hoped for more time with Carter, but it looked like that wasn't meant to be. They didn't even have a chance to say a private goodbye.

Maybe it was better this way. She'd said what she'd wanted to say to him on the beach that morning. A long goodbye would have only made it harder to leave.

Rose was chirpy and talkative the entire ride back to Hannah's place. Jeff was quiet, watching the road and just letting Rose do all the talking. They made a nice couple, and Hannah almost envied them how easy they were in each other's company. She wasn't sure she'd ever find a relationship like theirs. Or, maybe, she had, but she'd left it behind on an island she would never be allowed to visit again.

It was like something out of a fairytale. Or a nightmare.

Jeff slowed the car as they approached her house. For the first time since leaving the other island, he spoke.

"We'll still be keeping an eye on you, Hannah. I want you to know that. We won't just throw you to the wolves and forget you, but so far, it looks like you've escaped detection. Just go about your life as usual and gradually ease off the crutches over the next few weeks, as if your injury were healing naturally. You should be all right." He sounded so sure, she could almost believe it would be that easy. "I'm sorry we can't do anything about the extra surveillance in your house without alerting the wrong people that we've taken an interest. If you just go about your business as usual, the interest should ease off in a couple of weeks. We can alert you when the surveillance is gone, if you like."

"I'd like that very much," she told him. "I have no idea how you know what you know, but I trust you guys more than anybody else right now. You haven't steered me wrong, yet."

"See, Jeff? I told you she's smart enough to realize who the good guys are," Rose put in, making a funny face at her fiancé, as if her reaction was something they had already discussed.

"I didn't say she wasn't," Jeff said, in his own defense, turning the corner onto Hannah's block. "I'm just more cautious than you are, sweetheart."

"Caution is good in a soldier," Hannah said, belaying anything Rose might've said to argue. "I respect that."

"Rosie isn't quite used to the military mindset yet, I'm afraid," Jeff told Hannah in his clipped British tones.

He really was a handsome man, but Hannah could only really see Carter. The heartbreaker. At least...her heart might break. She didn't think his would, though he'd said he'd regretted that their time together had to end. That was something.

"Now, we won't walk you in. We're just dropping you off. Just two friends, giving you a lift home," Rose said. "Your house is safe, except for the extra bugs. Just do your thing and know that, even though you might be under surveillance from the bad guys, the good guys will be watching over you, too. Don't do anything too conspicuous, and all will be well."

"Is that a prediction from Madam Pythia?" Hannah said, teasing her new friend a bit.

"As a matter of fact, it is," Rose agreed, laughing along with Hannah. "And I'm usually right about these things."

Hannah let herself into her home a short while later, sorry to see Rose and Jeff pull away. Her last connection to the unit was gone, and she was on her own again. They said they'd be watching over her, but she had no idea what that really meant. Probably some sort of covert surveillance she would never even realize was there.

What good was that? She was grateful and all, to know that someone was looking out for her, but really, she wanted to see Carter again. She somehow doubted that was going to happen. Not the way he'd been talking. She recognized finality in a man's tone when she heard it.

Hannah made her way into her home, relying on the crutches that were just a prop, at this point, and headed for the couch. She would put her foot up, as she usually did after coming in, and watch the news. Back to her old routine.

While the weather report was on, her phone rang. It was Lulu, asking her to fill in at the mall again, the next day. Hannah agreed. Her dance card was currently empty, so she might as well help out her friend.

The next day, Hannah made a show of hobbling out her door and going to the mall, as she had any number of times since she'd come back from being overseas. She took up her position at the kiosk in the center of the mall and spoke with Lulu for a bit about various topics before she took off to run her errands.

It was a weekday. Slow time at the mall. Hannah had a few customers just after she got there around lunchtime, but after that, she just sat and had time to think over everything that had happened in the past few days. Her foot was encased in the boot she'd been given at the hospital weeks ago, but she didn't need it anymore, which was the only real proof she had that everything that had happened with Carter had been real.

She could move her ankle inside the ginormous boot with no pain. Every time she did so, she had to hide a happy grin. Her foot was better. Not just better, but healed completely. As her run on the beach the morning before had proven to her beyond the shadow of a doubt. That had been a magical hour—running with Carter on the beach just after the sun rose. What she wouldn't give for a life like that on a full-time basis.

But it was not meant to be. Danger dogged Carter's tracks, and she understood his reasons—the few he'd been able to explain and the few she'd extrapolated from his unspoken words. She respected his unwillingness to take her out of her normal life and into a world of danger and subterfuge, where they had to hide in plain sight and deal with enemies who wanted them so badly they were willing to follow them halfway around the world.

She didn't envy him that existence, but by the same token, he had a good thing on that island, with his unit. At least two of the other men had their women with them. Rose was with Jeff, and Casey was Hal's wife. They lived on the island with the guys, which was definitely not the normal way a military unit existed, but she suspected allowances had been made for them, since they had such an unusual situation with Rick and his abilities. Though why they'd been able to give Rose a job, when she was a self-proclaimed fortune teller, was still confusing to Hannah. Maybe they'd just devised something for bookkeeping purposes, so she could live on the island. Hannah would probably never know now.

She regretted that. She'd liked Rose. Casey, too, had been a very nice person, though a bit harder to get to know than Rose with her open manner. Hannah found she missed them, even after such a short acquaintance. Of course, she missed Carter the most.

She wasn't sure now, whether spending the night with him had been a good idea, or a really bad one. After making love with him, she feared she was now ruined for any other man. Maybe that would wear off in time, but right now, she yearned for Carter—and Carter, alone.

CHAPTER EIGHT

Carter disguised himself with a mustache and a bit of silver in his hair when it was his turn to watch over Hannah at the mall. They'd been taking it in turns to keep an eye on her, and Carter had personally thanked every member of the unit, and the captain, for taking the potential threat to Hannah's safety seriously.

Most of the guys in the unit had become really good at disguises over the past few months and were able to come and go from the island by taking reasonable precautions. Carter stationed himself as close as he dared to Hannah's position, using a convenient grouping of chairs in the center of the pedestrian area that were probably meant for men who accompanied eager wives on their shopping sprees. Just another older guy sitting, waiting, didn't draw any attention, and Carter had brought along a newspaper and a cup of coffee—a sure sign of a guy settling in for a long wait. Nobody took any notice of him. Not even Hannah.

Which was the way it was supposed to be, though it irked him to be so close to her and unable to speak with her. He knew it was for the best, but it didn't seem fair. He tried not to be too obvious in watching her. He didn't want to draw needless attention to himself, or to her, for that matter. He was here to blend in, not stick out, and looking at her too closely would not be *blending*. Not at all.

He'd been sitting in the same spot for almost an hour when his vigilance finally paid off. He'd pretended to read the paper, but in reality, he'd been listening closely to any conversation near enough that he could make out the words. The language didn't matter. When Carter heard languages he didn't know, they all made sense to him. That had been his gift from the turbaned man in the tower, in ancient Babylon. The gift of language.

All he had to do was hear the words, and he knew what they meant. Like the man pacing near his position, talking on the phone.

"She's here," he said, then sent through a photo he snapped of Hannah across the way. The language was familiar, but not. A dialect of a Middle Eastern tongue that Carter knew he had never heard before. But his gift made it perfectly understandable to him. "What do you want me to do?" the man went on, oblivious to

the fact that Carter heard—and understood—
every word.

The man listened for a few minutes then
disconnected the call. He made a gesture to his
friend, who was returning with two coffee cups
in his hands. The friend gave one to the first
man—Phone Boy, Carter designated the first
man in his mind. Coffee Guy sipped his coffee
while Phone Boy cursed.

"He wants us to wait until she finishes her
shift, then follow her out and take her in the
van back to his base." Phone Boy shook his
head. "As if we don't have better things to do
with our time than help that ass steal a
playmate. This woman is nothing. She's not
even pretty enough to make this worth our
while." Phone Boy turned away, clearly angry,
while Carter's anger rose.

He had to be cool, though. They couldn't
know he understood them or the vile way they
talked about Hannah. To him, Hannah was
more than beautiful. She was regal. A shining
example of what a woman should be. Tough,
tender, strong, supportive. Beautiful in a way
that was so much more than skin deep. To hear
her disrespected in such a way by this evil little
prick set Carter's teeth on edge. His fingers
twitched, wanting to make a fist and punch
Phone Boy's lights out.

But he couldn't. Not yet. Things were
unfolding and had to take their course, but
Carter promised himself he'd give Phone Boy
something to remember him by, if at all
possible, when the shit hit the fan. Satisfying

himself with that, Carter calmed himself and listened. He had to get every scrap of intel he could before he reported in to the guys. This sounded bigger than just a few goons abducting Hannah—bad enough as that was. This sounded like there was at least two separate groups involved. Phone Boy and Coffee Guy didn't sound like they were part of the same unit as whoever had been issuing orders on the phone.

Phone Boy suddenly spun back around to Coffee Guy. "You take first watch. Call me if she makes a move, but I doubt she will. This is going to take hours, and I've got better things to do. You watch. I'll be back later. Call if you need me."

And with that, Phone Boy stormed off. Carter wished he could follow the first man, but he dared not let Hannah—or her watcher—out of his sight. He settled in for surveillance and took out his own cell phone. He needed some backup, and he knew just who to call.

*

When the time came, Carter stayed behind Hannah, ready to assist while others from his unit acted as the take-down team. They waited until they were all out in the parking lot of the mall and the enemy made their move.

Hannah made her way slowly out the door of the mall on her crutches, Carter following behind. When she got through the first set of doors, he caught up and was right behind her as she made it through the small vestibule and out the second set of doors to the outside. If those two men were going to act, it would be within moments of her being outside.

Sure enough, a white van pulled up, and Phone Boy got out, heading straight for Hannah. Dan, another of Carter's colleagues, materialized right behind him. Carter saw Jeeves pull the driver of the van out onto the pavement and cuff him with zip ties before throwing him back into the vehicle—this time in the cargo area. Dan quickly immobilized Phone Boy and zip tied his hands behind his back.

A large black SUV pulled up behind the white van, and more of the unit piled out to support Dan and Jeeves. Hannah just stood there, motionless, probably in shock, and Carter came up behind her.

"Sorry, Hannah. They were plotting to abduct you, so we took them instead," Carter explained in a calm voice. Hannah whirled around to look at him.

"Carter!" There was joy, as well as relief, in her tone, which warmed his soul.

"I told you we'd be watching," he replied, smiling at her as Hal came up to them.

"Time to go, boys and girls," Hal said in a hearty voice. "If you'll trust us with your keys, one of my guys will drop your car at your place," he told her, holding out one hand.

Hannah gave him the keys, which had already been in her hand. Carter was glad she'd been prepared to get in her car and leave without fumbling in her bag for keys. It was a good precaution for anyone to take, but especially when she knew there might be trouble. Parking lots could be dangerous places, but Hal had already interfaced with mall security to allow the unit a bit of leeway here tonight.

"Since Hal's taking care of your ride, we get to go in the big black boat," Carter said, ushering her toward the large SUV that was idling behind the white van.

Dan drove the white van away while Jeeves took over the wheel of the SUV, and within moments, they were pulling away from the curb. The whole operation had taken less than five minutes, and they'd managed to avoid being seen by any civilians. They'd gotten away clean.

"Good job, fellas," Hal told them all once they were underway. "Sorry to sneak up on you like that, Sergeant Sullivan," Hal told Hannah. "Carter became aware of the threat only an hour or two ago, and we had to act without alerting you beforehand."

"That's all right," Hannah replied. "Thank you for keeping such a close eye on me. Were those two men really planning to kidnap me?"

"I'm afraid so," Carter replied. "I heard them talking, and it was clear they'd received orders from a paymaster of some kind to grab you after work tonight. We had to act."

Hannah felt an almost overwhelming need to

push into Carter's arms and seek reassurance, but she couldn't do that. Not in front of his commanding officer. Especially not when Carter had made it clear they were supposed to have parted ways for good. The fact that he'd been watching over her in the mall today sent a little shiver down her spine on several counts.

First, she was kind of shocked that she hadn't spotted him or at least felt *something*. Where was that famous sixth sense about being watched? She supposed she didn't have it. Or, maybe subconsciously, she knew it was okay because it was Carter. She had to scoff inwardly at her own justifications. She hadn't seen him at all, and that was on her. Of course, he was wearing a bit of a disguise. His hair had been silvered, and that mustache was something out of a Hollywood props department.

Second, she'd been totally unaware that the two men they'd captured had been plotting to kidnap her. Again, her awareness of her surroundings wasn't what it should have been. She wasn't in a war zone now, and she supposed her skills had dulled since being home, but she really should have been more aware of potential threats. Thank goodness Carter and company had been keeping as close an eye on her as they'd promised.

Which brought her to the third—and most pleasing—reason she was feeling shivery. Carter had been there for her. He'd been looking out for her, even when she was unaware of it. He'd kept his promise, and he'd kept her safe. She felt her heart melt at the thought. What a sweetheart of a guy. Her insides felt gooey with emotion as she thought of the way he and his friends had leapt into action to help her. They were all special guys, but in her book, Carter was the real hero of the hour.

It was well after dark when they finally arrived back on the island base. They'd spoken little during the trip, keeping the conversation general or pertaining to the recent action and what might come next. She didn't bring up anything personal. Not with the other guys in the vehicle listening. She hoped she'd get a chance for a private discussion—and more—with Carter later.

"Sergeant Sullivan, if you'll just wait here for a few minutes, we'll get the prisoners secured first," Hal said when they pulled to a stop in front of the barracks building she'd left just the day before.

Hannah agreed, and both Hal and Carter exited the vehicle, leaving her with the guy they called Jeeves for company. She knew his real name was Jeff, but it seemed most of the guys in the unit had nicknames that the other guys used regularly.

"If you don't mind my saying," Jeff spoke from the driver's seat, "you just need to be patient a little longer. Carter is conflicted about bringing you more fully into our situation, but after the events of the day, he's going to have to come to terms with the fact that you're in it, no matter how much he might wish you weren't."

"You mean that I'm in danger because of my

dealings with your unit?" She knew she was still missing something here, but she had hope she'd soon learn what it was.

"You could say that." Jeff met her gaze in the rearview mirror, and his blue eyes were spooky. "Look, you don't know everything, and when you do find out, Carter's probably afraid you might bolt. I know you won't." How could this man—this relative stranger—be so sure of how she would react? "Ah. I see this is one of those times Rosie warned me about where it might be better to say less rather than more." He blinked and released her gaze by looking outward, through the windshield. "Sorry. I'm still learning my way. As are we all. And you'll understand what I'm talking about later. Once you've had the briefing. For now, just know that there *will* be a briefing, and most of your questions will be answered."

"I'll take your word for it." She didn't know why her words made Jeff laugh, but he was still chuckling when Carter came back to the vehicle and opened the door for her.

"They're inside and under wraps," Carter told her. "Your turn."

Carter escorted her to the building. It was the first time they'd been somewhat alone since she'd left the island. She wanted to say things to him, but he preempted her by speaking first.

"I'm sorry, Hannah. None of us realized you were in that much danger. If we had, we'd have done things differently," Carter told her, his voice low and full of what sounded like regret to her.

"I'm just glad you were there," she told him. "And kicking myself for not realizing that you were."

Carter grinned. "You weren't meant to see me. I wouldn't have been doing my job if you had."

"I didn't realize costuming and undercover work were part of your military training," she dared teasing him.

"You'd be amazed the kind of things this unit gets up to," he told her.

They entered the building and found a small reception committee waiting for Hannah, consisting of Rose and Casey. They took her under their wings and cooed over her close call all the way to the mess hall, much to Carter's amusement. Hal came up beside him, and they watched the women retreat toward the back of the building.

"Your Hannah's made of stern stuff. I don't think Casey understands her, but she likes her, nonetheless," Hal reported.

Casey was a civilian all the way, like Rose, only without any sort of special ability of her own that made things with this unit a little easier to bear. Rose saw the future, like her fiancé, Jeff. Carter thought her extrasensory ability to know things had helped her settle into the group more easily than it would have been otherwise. Casey, on the other hand, had known Hal all her life. Hal had been her older brother's best friend since they were kids. It was obvious she loved every little thing about

114

Hal and trusted him with her life. She also knew his past and his motivations probably better than anyone else. That had to have helped her accept the strangeness that was their lives now.

By contrast, Carter and Hannah had only just met. They had no long history to draw on. She also didn't have any sort of extrasensory ability, so there was no common ground on that score. How could things work out between them without some kind of basis? Carter just didn't know, and it was a major stumbling block to any sort of future with her, as far as he was concerned.

"I'm glad Hannah's made friends," Carter answered his commanding officer and friend, noncommittally. Hal gave him a sharp look.

"I think we're going to have to bring her more fully into our confidence," Hal said in a serious tone.

Carter met his gaze. "Are you sure that's wise?"

"Jeeves and Rose seem to think it's a given," Hal answered, surprising Carter. "I've been on the fence about letting anyone else know too much about what happened to us, but I've also been talking to the base commander. Kinkaid is a man who knows how to keep a secret, and he seems to think that if ours is shared only with select people, chosen for their loyalty and honor, then we'll be okay. Our resident psychics agree." Hal sighed and rubbed a tired hand over his eyes. "I never expected any of this when I was tapped to command this special forward operating unit, but you're all adapting and overcoming, like good little soldiers, so I need to do the same. That includes the fact that I know you can't all go solo for the rest of your lives. You need wives and girlfriends. I'm lucky. I have Casey. But the rest of you... Frankly, I worry about you guys like you were my kid brothers or something."

"We appreciate that, Captain," Carter told his slightly commanding officer.

Carter was uncomfortably aware of the fact that Hal was talking about *wives*. Permanent partners for himself and the rest of the crew. Though, to be fair, after spending a day or two and just one amazing night with Hannah, Carter was also thinking along more permanent lines. And wasn't that scary as hell?

The rest of the guys came in, ending the conversation with Hal, and Carter wasn't sure if he was glad or not for the interruption. He did know he had a job to do, however, and it was past time to get started on that. Hannah was in good hands. Probably eating dinner with the other ladies, since it was well past suppertime. The guys had snacked on the go, and they'd eat later. The kitchen had been alerted to set up a cold buffet of sandwiches they could take out and nosh on later.

That was one nice part about having a base to work out of. Usually, when they were in the field, they had to make do with ration packs or whatever they could cobble together. Here, the base commander had given them support staff, including a kitchen crew that came in to feed them three times a day. It was cozy compared to what they were used to in the real world.

Carter and some of the other guys spent the rest of the evening trying to get information out of their prisoners. They were careful to use only English, not alerting the men they were holding to the fact that most of the team spoke various Middle Eastern dialects, and, in fact, Carter spoke them *all*. There wasn't a language he'd heard yet that he couldn't understand and speak, since his encounter with the djinn in the Tower of Babel. That's what he had concluded it was, after all. The other guys had different theories, but for Carter, that seemed the only thing that made any sense.

CHAPTER NINE

The colorfully-dressed man in that desert tower had to have been an ancient genie, but they hadn't had to rub a lamp or gotten three wishes. No, this magical being had had an agenda of his own, and after questioning them and learning what he'd wanted to know, he'd decided very deliberately to give them parting gifts without their knowledge or participation. Without even telling them. They'd had to figure it out the hard way when things started getting weird.

In Carter's case, he'd received the gift of language, hence his belief that the tower had been the actual Tower of Babel. It was almost a given that Rick, the doctor, would become a healer after their encounter, but some of the other guys' abilities were a bit more obscure.

Zeke, for example. He'd been one of the first into the tower, alongside Wil, who could now control the weather. Zeke was an archaeologist, and now, he had the ability to see the history of an object just by touching it. He was somewhat empathic with people, too.

He had come out with some freaky visions of things that had happened in Carter's childhood the one time they'd been working with the medical team stationed in the building next door. They had wanted to map the extent of Zeke's new powers, but they needed test subjects, and Carter had been volunteered. Zeke had just touched Carter's arm and had immediately been struck with a vision of Carter's childhood. An incident where he'd been beaten up by a group of older kids that had firmed his resolve to study martial arts and become as strong as possible, so that when he was older, he could stop bullies from hurting kids like himself.

Zeke had read the situation and every emotional nuance of Carter's nine-year-old self. It had been a little embarrassing at first, but Zeke hadn't spread the information around, and nobody had teased Carter about it after the fact. They'd all been learning to have even more discretion than they usually had to employ since getting these new powers.

Jeeves, for one, had agonized over how much to share of his visions of the future. Carter knew that was one of the reasons Jeff had sought Rose's help in the first place. She'd had the gift of clairvoyance all her life, and she

119

had more experience with knowing how much was too much for someone to know about their future. Since Jeff had been working with Rose, he'd been much steadier. Everybody had noticed it. Rose had been really good for Jeff, and most of the other guys envied them their relationship.

Hal, too, had paired up since returning to the States. It was a little different for them, of course. Hal had been in love with his best friend's sister for years. Casey had been in love with Hal, too. And Hal's gift had seemed so very dangerous to his life at first. He was the unit's strong man. He could lift incredibly heavy objects, and he'd even stopped a speeding car that had been about to hit Casey a few weeks back.

When they'd finally gotten together, they had a long history of friendship and love to build on. The guys all wanted Hal to find happiness—just in case his new power caused his death. Every time Hal used his super-strength, he went into a state of near-coma for hours afterward. The more strength required, the longer he needed to recover. They'd all feared that someday, the cost would be too high, and Hal wouldn't come back from the coma.

But reuniting with Casey—and marrying her shortly after—had seemed to stabilize Hal. Rose had foreseen a long and happy life for Hal and Casey, which had been a big relief to everyone in the unit. The guys were a tight-knit group, even if they had been put together based on their academic specialties. They'd bonded over time in the desert, and the tower experience had solidified that relationship. They were family now.

Zeke was sitting at a table, the prisoners' belongings laid out in front of him. The two men had been searched and left only with their clothing. No shoes, belts or anything that they could use to harm themselves or anyone else. They'd been put into separate rooms. Cells, really. Jeff had directed them to build these rooms when they'd been remodeling.

They'd had a lot of downtime when they first arrived back in the States and not much to do on the island. The base commander had made construction materials available and told them they could remodel their building as they saw fit, since it hadn't been used in years and needed *a good coat of paint*, as he put it.

It had needed a lot more than paint, but the guys had enjoyed doing the work. They'd turned their talents toward design and made a cozy nest for themselves. Jeff had insisted on at least two holding cells, and Hal hadn't argued. They'd all come to respect Jeff's foresight, and if he said they needed two cells, by golly, they were going to build two cells. They'd had the time and the materials. Plus, there was plenty of room in the old building they'd been given to work with.

They'd spruced up their own living areas first, but there were other parts of the building still under construction, and the guys worked on them as time allowed. If they were here long enough, they'd make a nice little home out of the old place, Carter knew. For now, they had just what they needed, including the two cells and a specially designed interrogation room, along with a few other specialized chambers that could be used for investigations.

This was one. An evidence room, of sorts, with a few instruments that might be useful in analysis. There was a microscope and some fingerprinting equipment. Carter didn't know what it all was. That wasn't his specialty. But other men in the unit had the training and scientific background that could prove useful in forensic analysis.

Zeke added his own supernatural ability to the mix. He'd been tasked to touch each of the items from the prisoners, to try to get a read on anything they might have been involved in recently. Like any good scientist, Zeke was being methodical in his approach, having directed the other guys to lay everything out, piece by piece, nothing touching anything else. He'd numbered every item, and Wil was standing by to take notes as Zeke handled each item in turn.

Hal and Carter were present to witness and as backup, should Zeke run into trouble. He'd had a couple of incidents overseas when he'd touched something really old or with a very violent past. He'd passed out a few times until he'd learned how to shut his senses down a bit so he wasn't so open to every little thing.

He'd be dropping all his defenses now, and he would be vulnerable. They didn't expect any of these items would trigger an episode, but it was wise to be cautious, because some things that looked innocent on the surface were hazardous underneath. They'd learned that the hard way.

"Nothing exciting from the jacket," Zeke reported. He'd started by touching the first item on their list, a new-looking designer jacket. "It was stolen from a high-end boutique last week."

"Classy," Hal murmured as Zeke moved on to the next item, a pair of sunglasses.

"These came from the mall kiosk. Also stolen when the clerk was distracted by this guy's accomplice. They're good at the snatch and grab," Zeke observed, putting the sunglasses down before touching a pen that had been in one of the men's pockets. Zeke started, jumping a little in his chair.

"What is it?" Hal asked.

"This was used to write some kind of...manifesto, I guess you would call it. Ranting and raving about the decadent West and the thieves that live here. Damn. This guy hates America and all the Western countries, really, but he's got a special hard-on for the U.S.," Zeke said before carefully removing his fingers from the pen.

Carter noted that Zeke's face was a bit pale. Whatever he'd seen or felt from that innocent-looking pen had been intense. Zeke paused a moment before going on to the wallet. The leather billfold had been emptied of its contents, which were elsewhere on the table.

"Stolen," Zeke mumbled, shaking his head. "Where's the cash?"

"Here," Wil answered, pointing to a spot on the table that held a wad of cash. "Why?"

Zeke replaced the wallet on the table before speaking. "Because I got a flash of something. The paymaster—whoever he is—paid this guy in cash last time, and I might be able to get something off the bills, if he still has any from that payment." Zeke took a deep breath. They knew from past experimentation that money was difficult since it changed hands so many times. Money always had a history, and it wasn't always pleasant. "Captain, could you hand those bills to me one at a time?"

"Sure thing." Hal put on gloves before handling the evidence and carefully handed Zeke one bill at a time, starting with the singles first and working his way up the denominations.

Zeke discarded the first few bills after cursory examination. "Nothing pertinent," he said before placing each bill on the table in front of him in a neat little pile. He did the same until they got to the first twenty-dollar bill. There, he paused.

"This bill is too young," he said at once. "Counterfeit." He closed his eyes. "Short history. Made recently. Nearby. I see the basement of a fancy house. A compound. Men and women working there on various projects."

"Identifying features?" Hal prompted quietly.

"Americans. All ethnic backgrounds. Not

what we expected. They're not jihadists. Not the way we think of them. Their goal is something bigger than politics. Bigger than religion. They want to destabilize the entire world. One of them is saying something about *human sheep*. Confusing the human sheep."

Carter frowned, shooting a look at Hal, but the captain was focused on Zeke. "Do you see any of them? What do they look like? Are there any animals in the vision?"

"Big dogs," Zeke said immediately. "No. Wait. Not dogs. Wolves." A shiver ran down Zeke's spine. "And a tiger?" Zeke's eyes opened, and he shook his head. "This doesn't make sense, Captain. I'm sorry."

"No, Zeke. It does make sense. You need to write down every last thing you saw, even if it seems crazy, and then tomorrow, we're all going to have a little meeting with the base commander. It's time we all got on the same page." Hal's expression was grim. "Stop for now. Make a full report on that last experience and have it to me before you turn in tonight. We'll do the rest of this tomorrow."

"What about the prisoners?" Carter had to ask.

"They'll be okay for the night. Wil, you've posted guards?" Hal asked the other man.

"Yes, sir. We're doing it in rotation. They will never be unobserved," Wil reported.

"Good man," Hal replied. "Then, there's nothing more to do but carry on. You two have your orders. Carter, with me. We're going to see how the women are holding up."

When Carter appeared in the doorway to the mess hall, Hannah was relieved. Not that she didn't like the other women, but they wanted to make a big deal out of the danger she'd been in, and it was something Hannah preferred to take in stride. She was a soldier, after all. She'd been in worse danger in the desert. A little mall abduction was nothing. Right?

The captain came in behind Carter and went straight to his wife, who just happened to be sitting next to Hannah. Carter held back a bit as the other men joined the group.

"I just want to thank you again, sir, for allowing your unit to come to my rescue one more time," she said, feeling it necessary to put her thanks out there again. These guys—Carter especially, of course—had gone above and beyond for her a couple of times, now.

"I'm glad we could help out, Sergeant." He looked at the table and seemed to note the coffee cups and absence of edibles. "Haven't you ladies eaten yet?"

"We decided to wait for you," Casey told her husband, placing her hand over his on her shoulder. When she looked up at him, it was clear to Hannah that they loved each other deeply.

Hal looked up at the other guys just entering the room. "Dan, can you and the others get the buffet trays out? The fridge should have everything we need."

"Sure thing, Cap'n," Dan replied, adjusting his trajectory to take him into the kitchen area.

A few of the other guys followed, returning in short order with platters wrapped in plastic cling wrap, which they deposited on the big table.

Jeff took his seat next to Rose, and Hal took the chair Casey had kept open for him. Hannah was pleased when Carter chose to sit next to her, reaching toward the middle of the table to unwrap the first of the platters. He let Hannah choose a sandwich before taking his own and passing the platter around the table. Plates were handed out the same way, and a tub with utensils was on the table for those who wanted them. Other platters with coleslaw, potato salad and other side dishes were passed around as well, and before long, Hannah had a plate full. It felt like a picnic, in a way. Cold cuts and creamy salads, soda and iced tea, which they dispensed from big pitchers at the center of the table.

The kitchen staff was long gone for the night, but the unit was eating a hearty meal that had been left for them. Hannah was impressed.

They all chowed down, enjoying the camaraderie of a shared meal. Hannah felt like it was all a bit unreal. She hadn't thought she'd ever see this room, or these people, again. Things had changed, once again, on a dime, and she had to adjust.

Wasn't the Special Forces motto something about adapting and overcoming? She had to do that. Her life had entered a strange zone, and she had to roll with the punches, such as they were. So far, everything had worked out in her favor, and she hoped the trend continued. She thought these guys had a lot to do with her good fortune. Especially Carter.

As dinner wound down and platters with pie and slices of cake were passed around, Hal spoke. "Today was almost FUBAR, but thanks to Carter and his special talents, we were able to save the situation," Hal said unexpectedly, garnering the attention of every person in the room.

Hannah was surprised. She hadn't thought the day was *effed up beyond all recognition*, at all. She supposed, if the bad guys had managed to abduct her, the term FUBAR would work, but they'd averted that. Quite handily, she'd thought. Apparently, the captain thought different.

What she couldn't figure out was what the captain had meant by Carter's *special talents* having to do with her rescue? What were his so-called special talents? And what made them— whatever they were—so different from the talents of the rest of these Special Forces behemoths? She dearly wanted to know.

She'd spent a lot of time thinking about Rick and Rose and all the others she'd met here, and something just wasn't adding up. There were all these hints that things were not quite as they seemed, but she had nothing concrete, except what she'd seen with her own eyes as Rick healed her foot and what little Rose had talked about when admitting that she was Madam Pythia from the new age shop.

"Now, we've all had a long day. You did

well, despite the short notice and shoddy intel," Hal went on. "I'm calling a mandatory unit meeting for eleven hundred hours tomorrow morning. All will attend, except those on guard rotation."

Hal stood, and the rest of the men stood out of respect. Casey stood as well, joining her husband, and Hannah stood because she was a soldier too, even if she wasn't in uniform. Rose just smiled, as if she knew something nobody else knew, which, if she really was clairvoyant, she probably did.

"We're turning in," Hal told them all. "Get an early night if you can. I expect big changes tomorrow." Hal left on that concerning note, with Casey by his side. He was very solicitous of his wife, in a way that made Hannah wonder if there was a reason he treated Casey like a fragile porcelain doll.

"Casey's pregnant," Rose told Hannah in a quiet voice once the couple had left the room.

"Do you read minds?" Hannah challenged Rose with a grin.

"Nope. Not me," Rose replied, "but it was pretty clear you were noticing the way Hal walks on eggshells around his wife. I think it's kind of cute."

It was, but Hannah wouldn't be caught dead calling the captain of a Green Beret unit *cute*, no matter the circumstances. She opted for a safer observation.

"He's very protective." Hannah felt proud of the way she'd skirted that conversational pothole.

"They all are," Rose admitted, her voice low, just between them. "They're good guys."

"The best," Hannah had to agree.

"Good to see you ditched the boot," Carter said near her ear while Rose answered something Jeff said to her.

"It's honestly good to be rid of it. Now that my foot is better, it was harder than I expected to have to hide it all day," she admitted. "Casey got me another pair of sneakers out of the storage cupboard. I'm going to owe you guys for all the gear I've been using."

"Not at all," Carter assured her. "The government is paying our way, and that includes supplies for anyone under our care." Dan and some of the others got up and started taking the few leftovers into the kitchen. "Want to take a walk on the beach?" Carter asked in a low voice.

"Thought you'd never ask," Hannah replied, feeling a bit playful. She was thrilled she'd have another chance to be here, in this magical place, with the man she...surely, not *loved*... Not so soon, right? But the man she admired above all others. Yeah, that felt right.

Though, she had to admit, the L word kept popping into her mind whenever she thought about him. Her more sensible side kept tamping that down. She hadn't known him very long at all. Love took more time to develop. Didn't it?

Whatever it was she really felt for him, it was intense. She wanted to be with him at all times. Even when they were just doing normal things. She wanted to be in his presence, hearing his voice, feeling the reassurance that he was there, and with her.

Gosh. When had she become so needy?

They left the others in the mess hall and headed for the dark beach.

CHAPTER TEN

Hannah felt the magic of the night surround them. A night she hadn't expected, alone with Carter with nothing but the wind, the waves, and the sand beneath their feet. The weather had picked up, and the waves were a bit more ferocious tonight than they had been the last time she'd walked this beach.

Their wildness echoed the wild impulses that drove her to make the first move with this enigmatic man. She didn't want to come across as easy, but she also wanted him to know that she was more than receptive to repeating their intimate encounter.

"You know," she began, trying to find the right words as they walked along, "even though someone tried to kidnap me, I'm kind of glad how things worked out. I felt really sad at the thought of never seeing this beach again," she told him, staring out at the water for courage. "And especially never seeing you again."

He stopped walking, and she went a step farther before realizing he'd halted. She stopped as well, and turned to face him in the faint moonlight.

"I didn't like it either, but it was the way it had to be," he said, his tone as mysterious as the dark night.

"Things have changed, though, right?" She needed to hear him say this wasn't going to end with the morning light. She wanted more time with him.

He sighed. "Yeah. Things have definitely changed." He moved closer to her, stepping right up into her personal space. "The opportunity for a clean break has come and gone."

He moved one hand to curve around her waist, almost tentatively, as if he was seeking permission. She didn't pull away. In fact, she moved closer, and his other hand moved to circle her waist as well.

"Did you really want that *clean break*, or did you feel it was your duty?" she asked quietly. It was important to her to know, even if his answer was painful to hear.

"The latter," he admitted, and she was able to breathe again. "Dragging you into this situation would have been irresponsible, but I realize I didn't drag you into anything. The enemy did. In one way, I'm relieved it happened. Seeing you at the mall... Watching over you, but unable to make contact... It was killing me to be so close and yet so far."

"And I keep kicking myself that I didn't see you," she admitted with a smile. "I thought I was more observant than that."

"Ah, but I am a master of disguise," he teased, leaning toward her so he could capture her lips with his own.

They kissed like lovers reunited—which they were—but there was a quality to their kiss that spoke of a longer or deeper commitment than they actually had. It was as if they'd been together a long time and then parted, only to reunite. If she didn't know better, she'd have thought they'd known each other for years, instead of only days.

Perhaps the danger of the situation had added something to their relationship. Compressed their timeline. Although...she'd been in dangerous situations before with men that she found attractive. The guys she'd worked with in the desert weren't bad guys. She could have easily dated almost any one of them, had they been free to do so. She'd never felt this unwavering pull toward any of them. She hadn't felt it toward any of her past boyfriends.

Only Carter. There was something so incredibly special about him...and she didn't just mean the fact that he was a Special Forces bad boy. Her family had more than one former Green Beret in it, and she wasn't overawed by the idea. No, it was Carter, himself. Something about him drew her like a magnet.

She wasn't fighting it, and, it seemed, neither

was he, any longer. Oh, he'd tried to break off their connection, but circumstances had been against him. She liked to think that he'd missed her in those hours of their estrangement, as much as she'd missed him, but she wasn't sure. Whatever the case, he was here now, with her. Kissing her like there was no tomorrow.

And she was *fine* with that. More than fine, actually.

He released her lips and kissed his way down her neck. Her eyes flickered open, and she gasped—not in pleasure, but in surprise. Carter drew back, seeming to understand the difference.

"What?" he asked, looking around.

"Eyes," she said in a soft voice. "Over there in the dune grass. Animal eyes, low to the ground, watching us."

"Seriously?" Carter turned to search the dune area behind him. "I don't doubt you, but it seems to have hidden or left."

"Maybe we should do the same," she said, a shiver running down her spine. Those reflective eyes had been spaced far enough apart that whatever it was that had been lurking in the grass wasn't something small.

"Hide?" Carter joked, looking at her, a smile on his lips in the moonlight.

She punched his shoulder. "Leave," she told him. "Let's go back to the barracks."

Carter slung his arm around her shoulders as they started walking back. "Your room or mine?" he asked in a low voice, his tone warming the marrow of her bones.

"Whichever is closer," she whispered back, and by mutual consent, they started walking faster. Much, much faster.

They managed to get to his room without anyone seeing them, and the minute the door closed, clothes flew every which way. He seemed as eager as she was to get down to bare skin. She'd no sooner slid her pants away and was completely naked, when he lifted her up and placed her on his bed.

First, he ran his hands all over her body, pausing here and there in the headlong rush toward pleasure. Then, he followed the same trail with his mouth, bringing the smoldering flames of her desire to roaring life. What he did after that, with both tongue and touch, made her want to scream in delight and anticipation, but she was mindful of the other people in the building and bit back her louder impulses. She moaned, though, quietly. And sighed. And grasped his body with fingers that tightened as he brought her to her first climax just by touch alone.

And, oh, what touches! He knew just how and where to run his hands, or fingers, or tongue, to bring her to exquisite tension. She came down from the high of climax to find him smiling.

"I guess you liked that," he whispered, just before he leaned down to nip at her lips.

She liked the smug light in his eyes, but she wanted to show him she could give as good as she got. Pushing at his shoulders until he figured out she wanted him to roll onto his back, she kissed him deeply until she had him just where she wanted him. Then, she drew back.

She straddled his thighs. Her feeling of power was strong as she rose above him. She reached for his hands and put them on her breasts, liking the way he followed her unspoken orders. Then, she reached between them and wrapped her hand around his hard cock. He was already wrapped and ready for her. He must've done that while she'd been otherwise engaged, drugged by his beguiling kisses.

Carter gasped as she squeezed him and found a rhythm that made him strain against her. Taking pity on the poor man, she lifted up just enough to take him inside her body, going slow, making it last. He felt so good. So hard and thick. So...perfect.

She encased him fully and then stopped for a precious moment to try to regain some semblance of control. She had almost come just from the act of joining. How was she going to last long enough to bring him with her next time?

It was a challenge she looked forward to undertaking. She just needed a moment to catch her breath.

Carter, however, had other ideas. He surged under her, moving his hands to her hips and back, supporting her as he rolled, taking her down to the bed, once more. He took over, positioning them facing each other, on their sides. It felt a little odd at first, but she liked the different feel of this position, and once he started moving inside her, she just hung on for dear life as fireworks seemed to go off inside her body.

Happy firecrackers. Crazy bottle rockets. Incendiary flowers of primal passion that went on and on, bursting and exploding inside her body. She felt Carter stiffen and heard his deep groan. This time, he was with her, and she felt a sense of completeness in the moment. In the man.

As far as she was concerned, being with Carter was the best experience she'd ever had with sex. Although, if she was being honest with herself, it felt like much more than just good sex. It felt like...forever.

Damn. She was in deep here and not sure where it would all lead. What had happened to playing it cool and protecting her heart? She didn't want to come out of this with a broken one and have to put together the pieces. She was getting too old for that. She'd suffered little heartbreaks with boyfriends from her youth, but she was older and supposedly wiser now. Right?

Then, why was she falling so hard and fast for a man that had told her flat out that he'd have broken things off forever had circumstances not worked against them? She was being a fool, but she didn't know how to stop. The feelings inside her weren't under her own control. It felt like something was driving her toward him, regardless of the fact that he'd have left her life forever, if only the enemy hadn't put her in their sights.

But she couldn't think about that now. Not while the afterglow was making her feel all warm and fuzzy and fatigued. No, she would sleep now, and think about things later. Preferably, much later.

She was aware of Carter wrapping her in his arms sometime later, cuddling close in the aftermath. He was such a great guy. The last thought she had before sleep claimed her was that it would be kind of nice to have this—to have him—in her life on a long-term basis. She could easily imagine waking up in Carter's bed when they were both old and gray. He'd smile, and his blue eyes would dance with deviltry, and each day with him would hold a new adventure.

It was a nice dream to carry into sleep.

*

After the morning exercise session, made all the sweeter by having Hannah, once again, running by his side, and later, sitting next to him at breakfast in the mess hall, Carter spent a couple of hours on guard duty. The prisoners were kept apart, in separate cells, and weren't talking, so Carter's skills didn't come into play, but he was glad to see them looking miserable and tired. The night guards hadn't bothered being quiet and had deliberately woken the men up every two hours when they changed shifts. It was a tactical decision, to keep the prisoners off balance. A little broken sleep wouldn't hurt them, and it might make them less guarded when they were questioned later.

Carter left Mike in charge of the prisoners at eleven hundred and headed straight for the unit meeting. Mike had been the unit's best interpreter until the tower. Now, he could read minds if he was close enough and the thoughts were strong enough. Nothing would happen with him on guard.

Carter wasn't too worried about what Hannah might be doing, either. Hal had probably made sure Casey would keep Hannah occupied while the guys ironed things out. Casey could be counted on in situations like that. She wasn't a soldier, or psychically gifted, but she was a stand-up gal who was steadfast and true.

The meeting was already in progress when Carter walked in, quietly taking a seat at the back. Hal and Jeff were up front, with Commander Kinkaid, the Naval officer who was in charge of the base. Carter was surprised by the other man's presence, but Hal knew what he was doing. He'd come to some kind of understanding with Kinkaid, Carter was sure, though he didn't know exactly what that entailed.

Hal nodded to Carter as he took his seat. He'd know that Carter had just been relieved of guard duty.

"What you're about to learn is something ranked right up there with our own secret, which I've briefed Commander Kinkaid on, fully," Hal said, much to everyone's surprise. "You'll understand in a moment why we can have such faith in Commander Kinkaid's discretion—and why he's trusting us just as much as we are him. The time for secrets, I am informed by Jeeves and his lady, is at an end here on this island." Hal looked around the room, meeting everyone's gaze in turn, to impress upon them what a big moment this was. Carter felt the impact of that gaze and began to feel a bit of apprehension regarding whatever it was they were about to learn. "Commander, you have the floor," Hal said, inviting the Navy commander to speak.

"I've not met all of you yet," the commander began. "I'm Lester Kinkaid. This entire island is my command, and you were given room here at the request of Admiral Morrow, to whom I report directly. This base was set up as a location where personnel with special abilities could recuperate, receive special training, and be housed when not on active field assignment. It is one of a very few special locations used for those, like you, who have abilities that are not common—or known of—in the regular human population. Everyone here has a secret. The fact that you all have similar, if not the same, kind of secrets, is why you were allowed to come here."

Carter wondered just what the commander was driving at. What other kinds of secrets could there be that would require this level of security and secrecy? He was drawing a blank.

"Sergeant Carter." The commander startled Carter out of his thoughts. "You and Sergeant Sullivan were observed walking along the beach last night. Did you see anything out of the ordinary?"

"Sir," Carter replied immediately. "Sergeant Sullivan thought she saw some sort of animal, but it was a flash from a set of eyes, quickly extinguished. Can't really be sure it was there. We didn't see any personnel at all."

"Oh, those eyes were there, all right. And they did belong to one of my personnel, as you put it. Only, the soldier wasn't in their human form when they saw you," Kinkaid said, much to Carter's surprise.

"Not in human form, sir? I don't understand," Carter said, hoping for clarification.

"Have any of you heard of shapeshifters?" Kinkaid put the question out to everyone. "I'm not familiar with all of your abilities, but one of you can manipulate matter, right? Walk through walls and such?"

"That would be me, sir," Dan spoke up from across the room.

"If you've seen him do that, then you can probably believe that other people have been born with the ability to change their forms from human to animal and back again," Kinkaid said, as if it was the most normal thing in the world.

"Like werewolves?" Zeke spoke up, his eyes wide.

Kinkaid nodded. "Not exactly like the old

horror movies, but yes, werewolves do exist."

"This is why I stopped you last night, Zeke," Hal put in. "You said you saw wolves. I immediately thought about what I'd learned from Commander Kinkaid. I forwarded your report to him about what you saw, and he's made some sense of it for us."

"Is everyone on this base a…um…shapeshifter?" Zeke asked the question that was foremost in Carter's mind.

The commander nodded. "As you might imagine, my people are used to having this island to themselves. We've had to curtail ourselves since you've been here, but now that you know about us, don't be alarmed if you see some apex predators roaming around. We're fully aware of our human sides when we are in our animal forms. I assure you, you're not in any danger from us, as long as you're one of the good guys." He smiled, but Carter felt the intensity of the predator that was likely behind Kinkaid's smile and felt a chill down his spine.

"We have the occasional seer among our people, and we're familiar with magic of many kinds, but some of you men have abilities we have never encountered before," the commander went on. "Don't be surprised if some of my people ask you about them. Some of us are big cats, and I'm afraid the curious streak in felines is one myth that is actually true." Kinkaid chuckled, and just like that, the tension in the room dissipated a bit. As he'd, no doubt, planned.

"Now, I understand from Captain Haliwell

that you plan to bring Sergeant Sullivan more fully into your confidence sometime today. I trust that you are the best judges of whom to share your own secrets with, but I ask that you do not reveal to her what I've just told you," Kinkaid went on. "I've got authorization to bring your unit in, but for anyone else, I'll have to clear it with my chain of command, which includes not just Admiral Morrow, but my Clan Alpha, as well."

"Commander, respectfully, what is an Alpha?" Hal asked.

"Each group of shifters has a leader of one kind or another. As an example, I'm the Alpha of my family group. It has to do with age, experience, and most of all, dominance. I'm also the local Alpha for every shifter on this base. My authority is absolute here. But my Clan has an overall Alpha to whom all others answer." Kinkaid paused a moment. "Like I said, I'm going to clear this with him before we go any further. Morrow has a lot of authority, but each species of shifter has their own Clan or Pack obligations, as well."

"We look forward to learning more about it," Hal told the man, "and we won't mention your people to anyone. This intel is compartmentalized within the unit, men," Hal told his people. "Until further notice."

"Yes, sir," they all answered, in unison.

Hal took Carter aside after the meeting adjourned. "I think you ought to tell her about us at lunch," Hal said, surprising Carter. "With all of us there to back you up."

"Are you sure that's wise?" Carter asked his friend and commanding officer.

Hal ran one hand through his hair. "Can't say for sure, but there's strength in numbers. I think she's less likely to think you're insane if we're there to verify your claims."

Carter nodded. "You've never steered me wrong, Captain. Thanks for the backup."

CHAPTER ELEVEN

Hannah sat next to Carter at lunch. She hadn't seen him since breakfast that morning, and she was glad to have him back by her side, if only to eat lunch together with the rest of his unit. Casey and Hal were seated across from them, and Rose and Jeff were to one side.

"We're going to try some more questioning of the prisoners this afternoon, Sergeant Sullivan," Hal told her as they neared the end of the meal. "I think you have a right to observe, considering you were their target. Also, it'll give you a chance to see some of the guys in action. Particularly Carter." Hal took a sip of his coffee and went on. "We're going to try some new techniques, and with any luck, Carter will get a chance to use his full abilities."

She wasn't sure exactly what the captain was

referring to, but she was glad of the chance to find out more about the men who had tried to abduct her. Carter and his buddies were all so mysterious sometimes. She definitely felt that there was more to the group than met the eyes. They were protective of their doctor and the miraculous things he could do, but it was more than that. They were protective of each other, too. As if every man in the unit had some sort of secret.

But, maybe, that was just her mind playing tricks. Sometimes, she let her imagination get the best of her. Maybe this was one of those times. Like last night on the beach and that flash of animal eyes she thought she'd seen. She hadn't wanted to tell Carter exactly how much that had startled her, but she was grateful when they'd left the beach to…whatever large animal that had been…and gone back inside.

Carter cleared his throat, redirecting her attention. "You know how Doc can heal, right?" he asked, his words somewhat hesitant. Hannah nodded, wondering why he was bringing that up. "Well, the thing is, Hannah, Rick wasn't the only one who was changed."

"Um…what?" Hannah asked, since he seemed to be waiting for an answer. In fact, as she looked around the table, everybody was looking at her, listening to their conversation.

"When we were scouting forward of operations in the desert, we encountered an ancient city," Carter launched into the story again, filling in a few more details this time. "It wasn't on any maps. There had been a notation about some ruins, but this place wasn't in ruins. It was empty, though." His gaze took on a faraway look, as if he was remembering. "And there was this big tower at the center of the city. I think it was the actual Tower of Babel."

"Not all of us agree on that point," Rick put in from the other end of the table.

"Agree to disagree," Carter said, flicking his friend a glance, and Hannah got the impression that this was an old argument. "The thing is," he went on, looking back at her, "we all were changed in various ways."

"How?" she asked, looking around the table, then focusing back on Carter.

"We went into the tower and there was a single man sitting on a small Persian carpet. I already told you some of this. Remember?" Carter asked and she nodded slowly. "That man asked us questions, and we talked for a long time, though none of us could say later exactly how long. We were all acting out of character—answering questions, instead of asking them, for one thing. It was like we were under a spell." Carter shook his head as he remembered. "Toward the end, he seemed to make up his mind, and then, he spoke a word over each one of us, separately. He got to me toward the end, or I would've been able to translate all the words. I know he said *sky* to Wil, and *earth* to Jake, though the language was completely foreign to me before the man spoke over me. I think what he said to me would have translated to *speech* or *language*, though I can't be sure."

"And that's probably the last time you'll ever hear someone say something you don't understand," Hal noted, a slight grin on his face.

"Do you mean that this man in the tower gave each of you a gift? Like Rick's healing ability?" The idea was fascinating.

Carter nodded. "In my case, I can hear any language, understand it, and speak it back like a native. Any language. Any dialect. Even the most obscure," he told her. "We've been testing it ever since we got back to the States, and I haven't missed a single one they've thrown at me yet."

"That's amazing," she told him, wondering at the implications of someone who could speak and understand any language. "What about if it's written down? Can you read them, too?"

Carter nodded, smiling just a bit. "Doesn't matter. Written or spoken. If it's a language, I can understand it."

"So, what did *sky* and *earth* mean to Wil and Jake?" she wanted to know.

"I can control the weather," Wil answered easily, smiling at her as she met his gaze down the other end of the table.

"And I can sense things in the earth. I think I can either start or stop earthquakes. Maybe both," Jake replied quietly. "We're still testing, but we have to go cautiously, because I really don't want to cause a tsunami via an undersea earthquake."

"Oh." She frowned. "Yeah, that would be a

problem."

Jake chuckled, as did Carter, at her response.

"We're still learning our way with these abilities, and the military has stashed us here until we figure out exactly what we can and can't do," Carter continued. "There's a team of doctors and scientists in the next building over, who have been working with us individually."

"You seem to be taking this well," Hal observed in a leading way.

"To be honest, I'm not sure what to think. I mean, I know Rick has got some kind of amazing medical mojo, but the rest of it... I just don't know." She shook her head. "No disrespect intended, but it all seems just a bit farfetched."

Lunch was pretty much over, and a few of the men got up and started to leave for their afternoon duties. Carter stood, as well.

"There's only one way to prove this to you, I guess. Let's go see the bad guys we caught. At the mall, they were speaking a somewhat rare dialect. I heard them and that's how I knew what they were planning. We've kept them apart since we brought them here. Today, we're going to put them together and observe," Carter told her as she stood beside him. Hal got up, as did a few others.

Hal kissed his wife and then came around the table to join Carter and Hannah, leading the way out of the mess hall. A couple of the other guys fell into step behind them.

"We questioned each of the men individually last night, in English. Neither said anything of value. In fact, they were both pretty tight-lipped," Hal told her as they walked along. "Plan is, to give them a meal and let them eat together in one of the rooms where we can listen in and observe. They probably think we won't be able to get a translation for whatever they say without serious effort and time. But Carter here, is playing the role of our secret weapon today."

Carter chuckled, as did Hal. Hannah was reserving judgment. The story they'd told her sounded incredible, but she'd seen things in her time that were inexplicable. Up to, and including, her experience with Rick and his healing of her ankle. She was willing to suspend disbelief and see where this might go. It sure would be seriously interesting if what they claimed was true.

They walked to the other side of the building and down a flight of stairs. There was a holding area down there that she hadn't expected. Built into the basement was a set of cells with connecting rooms that looked like they could be used for interrogations or even just conferences. These guys had quite the facility at their command.

Hal led the way into an observation room while the other guys moved the prisoners around. He took a seat as Carter politely offered another chair to Hannah then took the empty chair at her side.

"They can't see us," Carter told her. They were facing a very large window that looked in on the conference room. "The mirror on their side is one-way and the whole thing is made of very thick Plexiglas. They can't break through, even if they had a firearm. It's bullet-proof. Their table is also bolted in place," he went on.

"And their chairs are flimsy plastic that couldn't make a dent in the wall without some serious effort," she finished for him. "I see you've thought of everything. I wouldn't have considered using cheap plastic patio chairs."

"We're on a budget," Hal said, his quick wink indicating he was teasing.

Hal turned on a computer screen and started tapping on the keyboard. He brought up what looked like feeds from video cameras that must be hidden in the halls. Looking over Hal's shoulder, Hannah could see the prisoners being escorted, one at a time, from their cells, into the conference room. A platter of sandwiches was already laid out on the table, alongside a small stack of napkins and some bottles of water. There were no utensils, but then again, they didn't really need them with sandwiches. Smart.

They brought the first prisoner in, and he looked around suspiciously before his gaze landed on the sandwiches. He went to the table, pulled out a chair and started picking through the available sandwich choices. He was already eating when the door opened and the second prisoner was let in. The first man stopped eating to stare at his cohort.

"Contestant number one is the guy who was driving the van. He appeared to be subordinate to contestant number two at the mall yesterday," Carter said.

"He stopped eating when number two entered," Hal allowed. "I suspect we'll see more subservient behavior, confirming your observations."

Sure enough, when the second man nodded, the first guy resumed eating. Number two, as Hal had called him, sauntered around the room, looking at everything before finally taking the only other chair and seating himself next to his fellow. He pulled the tray of sandwiches over in front of himself and made a few selections. The other man handed the newcomer a bottle of water, even opening it for him, like he was a servant.

"Bingo," Hal muttered. "You definitely read that right, Carter. Number one is the lackey. Number two is calling the shots."

"Unless they're acting," Hannah offered with a shrug.

"Point taken, Sergeant," Hal told her with a nod, "but Carter observed this dynamic even before the bad guys knew we were watching, so I'm betting we have it right."

Hannah nodded. They'd clearly dealt with prisoners, and evaluating people, a lot more than she had. She would watch and learn.

"Now, if they would just start chatting," Carter said, leaning forward to study the scene before them.

Hal had turned on the microphones that had to be hidden in the other room and adjusted the volume even before the prisoners had been let inside. They could hear everything in the other room from the scraping of chairs against the floor to the surprisingly loud chewing as the men ate. Finally, they began to speak to each other, tentatively.

"Here we go," Carter murmured as he began to listen.

Hannah sat back and watched. The language didn't sound like anything she'd ever heard before, but Carter seemed to be making sense of it. He listened closely as the men began to speak more freely.

"These guys aren't foreign intelligence agents," Carter said after a few minutes of watching the men through the one-way glass. "They're members of a terrorist sleeper cell that was planted here years ago, and recently activated. They keep talking about the packages and how glad they are that they had finished wrapping them before the jackass from the government that's paying them told them they had to watch the kiosk in the mall for the woman with the bad foot."

Hannah gasped, and Carter put his hand on her shoulder in a show of support.

"So, they were definitely sent by someone else. A paymaster of some kind?" Hal asked.

"Definitely. They're stringers who were getting a stipend from a foreign government, but now that they're actively planning a mission, they resent being pulled away from it to help the government that's been paying their way all these years," Carter commented, not looking away from the two men who were still talking in their rather unique dialect.

"What's their mission? Have they said?" Hal asked.

"Not yet. Just the packages and wrapping them. Wait." Carter listened closely for a moment. "Someone named Hamid is going to deliver the packages tomorrow morning, before the roads close for the festivities." The men in the other room laughed, and it was an evil sound. "They're joking about how much bigger the festivities are going to be than the stupid Americans think."

"Oh, no." Hannah shook her head. "There's a parade tomorrow. Right down Main Street in my town. To celebrate the little league team winning the state championship."

"That's it." Jeff spoke up from the doorway he must have opened moments before. "I was coming to tell you that Rosie and I were seeing explosions along a suburban street and lots of people lining the sidewalks. The bombs were stashed in flower pots along both sides of the road. Homemade bombs, full of shrapnel. Nails and ball bearings."

"Not on my watch," Hal muttered darkly, then turned to Jeeves. "We need to confirm the location with a landmark or something."

"There was an old white church, like something you see in New England, and a triangle of land with a statue," Jeff said without hesitation.

Hannah got out her phone and started tapping furiously, then turned the phone to face the guys. "This statue?" she asked.

Jeff nodded. "That's the one."

"That's my hometown," she confirmed. "The statue was put up twenty years ago. A donation to the town by a world-renowned artist who was born there. It's one of a kind."

"All right, that's enough for me," Hal stated, rising from where he'd been leaning on the corner of a desk. "Let's call in our intel. We'll stop this attack before it has a chance to start."

The room started emptying out, leaving Carter sitting at the table, still listening intently.

"There has to be something more we can do," Hannah said, worrying about the situation.

"Hal will report it, don't worry. These guys won't get away with anything," Carter said, his attention still on the men on the other side of the glass.

Hannah didn't like the casual attitude. People were in danger. Real danger. Why wasn't anybody doing anything about it?

*

At dinner that night, Hal sat next to Hannah, Carter on her other side. She was worried enough about tomorrow to have tried to call Lulu but hadn't been able to get through to her friend. In fact, Hannah's cell phone wasn't working at all out here on the island, no matter where she was. She'd tried every spot she knew in the building and even taken a short walk outside to the beach, but she had no bars. No signal. No way to warn her friend.

And the casual attitude of the men really

bothered her. If they weren't going to do something, then Hannah was going to have to find a way to do it herself. Nascent plans were percolating in her mind, but she wasn't sure if she'd have to act.

"Good work today with the prisoners," Hal complimented Carter, who sat on Hannah's other side, as they ate dinner. "We'll try the same trick again, tomorrow and see what else we can learn."

"Tomorrow?" Hannah asked, trying to hide her concern. "What about the parade?"

"We've given the intel to local police and the feds," Hal told her. "They gave me assurances that they would act to neutralize the threat and capture the last member—or members—of the terrorist cell."

"So, that's it? You just pass along the information and hope they get it right?" Hannah couldn't help the anger in her words, though she tried hard to bite it back.

"I understand how you feel, Sergeant," Hal told her patiently, "but as you know, we're not able to work officially on U.S. soil. A little thing called the Constitution prevents us from acting directly."

"That didn't seem to stop you from acting in the mall," she muttered. "Either time."

"Point taken." Hal accepted the hit. "But, in the normal course of events, we can't act with any official sanction. Both times we were in the mall, we were off-duty and acting as civilians, though I grant you, there's a fine line there that may have been crossed a bit. Suffice to say, we're not going to do it again. At least, not on purpose. And running an op to stop the terrorist plot against the parade route would be just a bit too deliberate and way out of bounds. We've been warned off and ordered to hand this over to the local authorities, and I have done so. I'm no happier about it than you, but that's the way it has to be."

Unable to eat any more, Hannah stood. "I understand, Captain, though you'll have to forgive me for not liking anything of what you've just said. Please excuse me. I've had a long day, and I'm going to retire."

She couldn't look at Carter, lest he guess what she had in mind. She could feel his gaze drawing her like a magnet, but she had to be strong. If she looked at him, she'd never go through with her half-formed plan, but she just kept thinking of Lulu. She knew for a fact that Lulu was going to be at the parade because her nephew was marching in it. For both their sakes, Hannah had to act. She had to at least try.

Carter stood to go after Hannah, but Rose motioned for him to sit. "Let me," she told Carter. "We've foreseen a bit of what this is about. I need to talk to her anyway. Jeff will fill you in on the rest."

Carter sat, unhappily, and waited for Jeff to speak. All eyes were turned on the clairvoyant among them, as they waited for his report. Rose followed after Hannah, and Carter hoped Rose would be able to calm Hannah down. She'd been so angry. Rightfully so. She'd hidden it well, but not from him. He knew her too well, by this point. He could see the way she was holding back her anger.

"Rose and I have been debating how much to tell you all. We both agree, we're at a very tricky juncture," Jeff told them, frowning. "If one of us goes off half-cocked, there'll be hell to pay." Everyone looked at Carter.

He wanted to growl. "I won't allow Hannah to be put in more danger."

"And that's part of the problem," Jeff confirmed. "She's got a pivotal role to play, and we have to let her play it."

"I don't like the way that sounds," Hal interjected. "Are you saying we have to let her become involved in the terrorist take-down? I have explicit orders against our unit having anything to do with tomorrow's activities. There will be feds and local law enforcement all over the place. We couldn't act, even if we wanted to. No way our unit would go unnoticed."

"Which is why we can't all go," Jeff confirmed. "But Hannah can. And Carter can follow. That's it. Just a couple out to help their friend. No official action. Nothing to hide from the locals, if you do things right, Carter." Jeff gave him a knowing look. "But the hard part for you is that you can't tell her. She has to act on her own, and we have to get out of her way. Let her set up the events that will need to unfold in a precise manner."

"I hate it when you talk in riddles," Carter

growled at his friend. "And I hate it even more that you sound like you want me to let Hannah walk, knowingly, into the middle of a terrorist attack."

Jeff shook his head. "I'm afraid that's exactly what we're asking you to do."

The *we* brought Carter up short. "You both saw this? Not just you?"

Jeff nodded. "Rosie and I both saw it. We discussed it before we came in for dinner and arrived at this plan of action. I can't tell you more than I already have."

"I don't like this at all," Carter muttered.

"Your objection is noted," Hal said, eyeing Jeff and Carter with a sly look. "But, since the desert, have you ever known Jeeves to steer any of us wrong?" Hal had a point. "I think we're all going to have to trust him on this."

CHAPTER TWELVE

Hannah was fuming as she walked down the hall to her room. She had reached her door by the time Rose caught up with her. Hannah had known the other woman followed but hadn't wanted to pause too close to the mess hall. She didn't want to give Carter an opportunity to try to stop her.

He hadn't come after her. Part of her was angry that he hadn't even tried, while another part of her was glad because she didn't think she'd be able to carry out her plans with him watching. Those plans were half-formed, at best, but she had been taught the value of thinking strategically. She tried to never go into a situation without having thought through as many of the possible outcomes as she could. Up to and including possible exit strategies.

"I know what you're going to do." Rose's voice came from behind Hannah as she paused at the door to her room. "I really am clairvoyant. The Madam Pythia routine was for real," Rose told her. "It's why Jeff sought me out. It's why I was targeted."

At this, Hannah turned to look at Rose. "Targeted?"

"That day at the mall. I was the one the gunman was following. I'm the one that led the gunman to the team. Jeff had come to warn me, almost too late," Rose revealed. "I had agreed to meet him for coffee at the mall café. That's where the enemy caught up with us both. Apparently, the enemies of the unit had been watching me, as a conduit to Jeff. He has the same ability I do." Rose shrugged. "Well, similar. I've that had it all my life. Jeff is still learning his abilities and limitations. So far, he seems to be limited to seeing only the future, while I can sometimes see the past."

"Why are you telling me all this?" Hannah wanted to know. Now that she had decided upon a course of action, she didn't want to stand around talking. No matter how interesting the topic.

"So you'll know that you weren't the only one in the crosshairs. Casey didn't come to be here via an easy path, either," Rose revealed. "We're here because we want to be here. With our men." Rose shifted her weight to lean against the wall next to Hannah's door. "We gave up the outside world, for now, until this situation can be resolved. And, before you ask,

I have foreseen that it will be resolved, but the path is tricky, and long-term. Everything has to go right in order for the best possible outcome. And part of that is happening, right here, right now."

"You mean the parade situation?" Hannah was intrigued by what Rose might have seen.

Rose nodded. "Most importantly, your response to it."

Hannah debated internally. She would not reveal her plans to anyone at this point, but something about the look in Rose's eyes told her she might not have to actually say anything. Rose saw the future. If Hannah believed that, it would be easy to also believe that Rose knew what Hannah intended to do.

"I hope you're not going to try to stop me," Hannah said in a low voice.

Rose straightened from her leaning position. "Far from it."

"Then, what?" Hannah turned fully toward the other woman to meet her gaze.

"I'm going to help you get off the island." Rose shocked Hannah with that pronouncement. "Thing is, you need to be at that parade. I've seen that much. The whole unit can't be there, but you can. I believe your presence will help unravel the entire terrorist cell, if all goes as I have foreseen. Sometimes, it doesn't." Rose made a face full of consternation. "We each just have to do the best we can. And, Hannah, your best is very, very good. I've seen it, and the rest of the guys will realize it soon enough."

"I'm not sure whether to thank you for your confidence in me or run away screaming," Hannah admitted with a small grin.

"Well, let's work on the running away part. There's a small window of opportunity to get you off the island, and you need to take it. Want anything from your room?" Rose asked, all business, suddenly.

"Not really. Just the dark hoodie, I guess, and my purse," Hannah replied.

"Get them, now. I'll be back in a minute. Wait here for me," Rose said, already walking down the hall toward the room she shared with Jeff.

Hannah went into her room and got her stuff, looking around to see if there was anything else she didn't want to leave behind, but she knew she had to travel light, and most of the stuff in the room had been given to her out of the storeroom here on the base. She had her belongings and was out in the hall again, in time to meet Rose, who was just emerging from her own room, down the hall.

Rose beckoned her over and hefted a dark knapsack. "I took the liberty of packing some things for you. Jeff helped," she explained, handing the small bag to Rose. "Just some equipment we thought you might need."

"Thanks," Hannah replied, wondering what they could possibly have packed for her, but there was no time to check it right now. She'd look later, when she was across the water and back on Long Island.

"Now, the kitchen staff will probably be

ready to go soon. They take the garbage with them, and it gets ferried across the water for disposal on Long Island a few times every week. Tonight's the night. Jeff and I have set aside an empty dumpster, just for you. Get inside, they roll you aboard the boat and carry you across. You get out on the other side and go on your way. Just be sure you get out as soon as you're back on land, or you'll has a very uncomfortable trip to the dump." Rose giggled, and Hannah had the scary feeling that the other woman wasn't taking this seriously enough.

Hannah hadn't been on the island long enough to really learn its rhythms, but she had made note of the few things she had observed. One of those things had been the kitchen staff going about their business. Hannah suspected Rose was right about the trash schedule. It was a reasonable way to get off the island, without too much fuss.

Hannah nodded at Rose. "Thanks for your help with this."

"Don't thank me yet," Rose said, serious once again. "You've got a difficult task ahead of you. Don't fail."

"I don't plan to," Hannah assured the other woman.

They crept outside to where the trash bins were kept. Rose acted as lookout while a last of the kitchen garbage was loaded into a dumpster. The staff member went back inside for a moment, and Rose gestured urgently to Hannah.

"Now's your chance," Rose urged. "The blue

one on the end. It's only half-full, and its paper recycling. Nothing too gross."

"Thank heaven for small mercies," Hannah quipped before making her way toward the big blue dumpster at the end of the row, Rose at her side, helping.

They opened the large hinged lid together. Rose held it while Hannah jumped inside. Before Rose replaced the lid, she apparently had one last thing to say.

"Carter didn't follow you out of the mess hall, because Jeff held him back. This is your mission. Your task. If Carter comes to help, it won't be until tomorrow. We'll keep him here until then," Rose cautioned her.

"Thanks for telling me," Hannah replied before the lid closed over her head. She tested it, making sure she could open it from inside was little difficulty, then settled back to wait.

In the dark of the bin, alone with her thoughts, Hannah was glad Rose had given her that last bit of information. She'd hated the idea that Carter hadn't even tried to console her. Knowing his teammates had kept him away, oddly, meant a lot to her.

After one of the strangest nights of her life, Hannah showed up at Lulu's doorstep just after dawn the next morning. She had been jostled a little on the trip over from the smaller island but had come out of the experience otherwise unscathed.

Lulu was one of her oldest, and dearest, friends. She, thankfully, didn't ask too many questions before inviting Hannah inside.

"What's going on?" Lulu asked as she shut the door behind Hannah.

"Too much to explain easily, and a lot that I just can't explain," Hannah replied.

"Come into the kitchen. I'll make coffee." Lulu was in her robe, and Hannah knew she'd awakened her friend with the doorbell.

"Thanks." Hannah followed Lulu into the kitchen and sat down at the table while Lulu bustled around fixing coffee. "You still planning on going to the parade today?" Hannah asked.

"Sure. My nephew is part of the team. I have to be there," Lulu replied automatically.

"I wish you wouldn't."

Lulu turned to stare at her. "Why?" Lulu's eyes narrowed.

Hannah sighed. "There's a threat against the parade that I heard about, but they're not publicizing. Terrorists."

"You're serious." Lulu didn't react wildly. She had always been a thoughtful soul.

"I'm afraid so."

"This has something to do with the mall gunman?"

Lulu was too clever by far. "How did you figure that?"

"Oh, come on. I know that mall, and I know everyone who works there. I've heard the truth about what happened, not the story that was on the news," Lulu scoffed. "The security chief asked me, just the other day, how you were doing, since you were right in the middle of it."

Hannah hadn't really thought about the fact that other people at the mall had seen the action behind the kiosk during the gunfire. She had thought that nobody had noticed in the frenzy of the moment. Then again, Carter had stayed with her even after the rest of his unit had exited the mall. Apparently, someone had noticed and had mentioned it to Lulu.

"I guess he figured you'd actually *told me* what happened," Lulu went on, her tone a bit hurt.

"It wasn't a big deal," Hannah said automatically. "I didn't want to worry you."

"Worry me! Girl, you've been harder to track down lately than you were in the desert. And now, you show up here at the crack of dawn, without your crutches. I thought you were never going to walk right again, but you look good as new." Her tone turned a bit accusatory. "What the *hell* is going on with you lately? Was the injury all some big ruse? If so, why? And if not, what in the world happened?"

"That's a lot of questions," Hannah said, to buy time. She wasn't sure how much she could tell Lulu, though she trusted her friend with her life. Remembering that made it easier. "Okay. First, the injury wasn't a fake. I can't tell you how, but I found a cure the other day, and I have to keep it under wraps to avoid drawing attention to the person who helped me. Can you promise not to give me away?"

"You know I never would." Lulu looked affronted.

Hannah nodded. "I appreciate that. Same

goes for me, you know."

"I know. It's why we're besties, even if you go off to foreign countries for months on end without a word." Lulu grinned, and Hannah reciprocated. After a moment, she went on.

"Second, I can't really tell you where I've been lately. That would break a confidence I promised to keep," Hannah explained. "It's nothing bad. In fact, it's related to my job, in a way."

"Your job as an employee of Uncle Sam?" Lulu asked, arching one eyebrow in surprise. "So, you're saying—in a roundabout way—that this has something to do with the military." It wasn't a question, and Hannah didn't reply. Lulu went on, surprising Hannah with her knowledge. "The head of security at the mall mentioned the team that had been shot at was military. Special Forces, he said, as if I already knew. He said he wouldn't have mentioned it otherwise, but since it was my kiosk that was in the middle of everything, he figured I already knew. Of course, I didn't because my bestie didn't see fit to tell me."

"I've explained that it's job-related for me. I could get in serious trouble for even saying as much as I have," Hannah told her best friend.

Lulu was silent a moment while the coffee maker dripped. The aroma of freshly brewed coffee began to fill the air, making Hannah impatient for the machine to complete its work.

"So...terrorists are targeting our parade, huh?" Lulu seemed accepting of the concept, her expression thoughtful. "You going to stop them?"

"I'm going to try."

"What about those soldiers? Can they help?"

"Not legally," Hannah replied, shaking her head. "They passed on the information to the local cops and the feds, but I'm not sure what will happen from there. I needed to come here to warn you."

"You were with those soldiers yesterday? Is that why I couldn't find you anywhere?" Lulu accused.

Hannah nodded again. "Part of the group targeting the parade tried to kidnap me the other night when I left the mall. One of the soldiers helped me." She wouldn't go into more detail than that. She'd probably already revealed too much as it was.

"Kidnap you?" Lulu's voice rose. She took a deep breath before going on. "Why was that soldier hanging around? It's awfully convenient he was there to help."

"Apparently, they've been watching over me since the mall shooting. Because I was in the middle of it, they wanted to make sure there were no repercussions for me after the fact." It was too much to explain about the enemies of the unit, so she glossed over that bit. "As it turned out, they were right to keep an eye on me."

"Thank goodness," Lulu agreed. "So, they're the ones who fixed your ankle?" Lulu sent her a knowing look.

"I'm not at liberty to say," Hannah said in a pompous tone that made them both smile. "I'm sorry, Lulu. We really just need to leave that topic alone."

"All right," Lulu agreed, giving Hannah a sideways wink. "I'll be good. For now."

"Does that include not going to the parade?" Hannah was hopeful but knew Lulu could be really stubborn.

"Sorry, no. But it does include me loaning you a wig and a suitable disguise, since you don't have your crutches. I assume you don't want anyone to recognize you without them for now, right?"

Hannah smiled. "Exactly right. I knew I could count on you. Plus, my house is bugged."

"Your house is what now?" Lulu did a double-take.

"Yeah, I know." Hannah sighed. "Remember those cameras and motion detectors you put upstairs and in the basement for me? Apparently, I wasn't the only one who decided to put that kind of thing in my home." Hannah shook her head. "Which is why I opted to come here, instead of going back to my place."

"You do seem to have gotten yourself involved in some serious stuff here, Hannah. Are you sure this is safe?" Lulu looked concerned.

"Safer than doing nothing. I mean, I was just minding my own business, and two goons tried to abduct me. I'd rather be doing something about it, rather than waiting for someone else to fix things...or not." She sighed. "I need to be part of the solution, here."

Lulu nodded slowly then turned to get mugs

out of the cabinet as the coffee maker neared the end of its brewing cycle. "I can understand that. I just hope you're not in over your head."

"Me too," Hannah muttered as Lulu poured coffee for them both.

*

Carter was incensed at being held back. He'd wanted to go after Hannah the moment she left the mess hall last night, but his clairvoyant friends had basically tied his hands. Jeeves and his lady had been adamant that Hal keep Carter on the island until this morning.

Carter had seethed and made plans all night long. He wasn't sure where Hannah would be, exactly, but he would start with either Lulu or the parade. Chances are, she'd be with her friend or along the parade route somewhere. Possibly both.

He went armed, but in civilian clothing. Jeans. Tee shirt. Motorcycle boots. He also got his Harley out of the base garage and drove that around Long Island on his quest. It hadn't been practical to use his bike for his previous excursions involving Hannah, but today, he liked the flexibility of being able to go just about anywhere on the two-wheeled monster.

Another good thing about riding the bike was the helmet that concealed his face. It was the best disguise he'd used yet. At least while he had the helmet on. He'd brought mirrored sunglasses and a ball cap for when he wasn't riding.

Carter knew Lulu's address. It was part of the background information they'd collected on Hannah after the mall incident. He drove by Lulu's first, but when he went up to the door, nobody answered. It wasn't too long until the parade was supposed to start, so he assumed they were there, somewhere along the parade route. Carter swung back onto this bike and headed for the downtown area parade route.

He had to find Hannah before something bad happened. He just had to. There was no other choice.

*

Hannah and Lulu were walking the entire parade route, looking for anything suspicious. So far, they'd seen nothing, except some overzealous gardeners were digging like crazy in all the giant planters along the street. There were a few police cars who had already closed off the road to vehicular traffic, even though the parade didn't start for an hour.

"Usually, they just close off the road to cars a little at a time, just before the parade gets to each major road. This is odd," Lulu said quietly to Hannah, as they pretended to be walkers out for a morning's exercise.

Lulu had loaned Hannah a black wig and trendy wide headband, plus big sunglasses that obscured most of her face. She also wore one of Lulu's jogging outfits. It was a bit large on

Hannah, but that was helpful in disguising her exact shape, as well. Hannah was confident that nobody would recognize her from a distance and probably not close up, either.

"Remember those things I told you they hid along the roads when I was in the desert?" Hannah was careful not to say anything overt, in case someone could hear her talking.

"The roadside—"

"Yup," Hannah cut Lulu's words off. The last thing they needed was for someone to hear the word *bomb* and jump to the wrong conclusion about them. "That's what I heard was supposed to happen here. Those guys," Hannah made a small gesture toward the men digging in the planter they were passing, "are probably looking for that kind of thing."

"Those are special dogs, aren't they?" Lulu said quietly. Hannah had also noticed the obvious working dogs who were sniffing the planters before and after the men started digging.

"If they'd found anything, I think there would be a lot of barking, and a whole lot more action. For one thing, they would evacuate civilians from the area and not let people on the street," Hannah mused as they walked along.

At that moment, a dog started barking. Hannah froze, as did Lulu. She looked back, but it wasn't one of the trained bomb-sniffing dogs. It was someone's pet, on a retractable leash, running around like a crazy thing while its owner stopped to chat with a friend. Hannah resumed walking.

"It's not like we're on edge or anything," Lulu quipped, and they both laughed. The small joke eased the tension a bit, and Hannah was thankful Lulu had insisted—against Hannah's advice—on coming with her this morning.

CHAPTER THIRTEEN

Carter had to leave his bike at one end of Main Street. The local police had already closed the street to vehicles not involved in the parade. They'd done it early, Carter realized. Much earlier than such things were usually done in a busy suburban area. Traffic was being re-routed around the parade route, but things were already backing up and would only get worse as the day wore on. Carter found a safe spot for his bike and set off on foot, leaving the helmet with the Harley and putting a baseball cap on his head, instead.

There were a lot of people walking along the street at this hour. Some were just shopping in the little stores that lined the road. Some were setting up lawn chairs for the best possible vantage points from which to watch the parade in comfort. A few vendors were selling hot dogs and other food items from carts that had been set up at the edge of the road, giving the place a carnival atmosphere that would only increase once the parade began.

He saw the dogs and the rather obvious police and federal agents looking into every flower pot and crevice. He wasn't impressed by their actions, but he knew just by looking that the dogs hadn't found anything yet, so that was something, at least.

But had they pre-empted this attack, only to make the cell try something else, later? They had the bombs. They would try to use them. Fortune had smiled on them this time, because Carter had been able to understand that the men they had in custody were up to something, and Jeff and Rose had foreseen the event. That might not happen again. If the terrorists were scrambling to find a new target for their ready-to-go bombs, there might be no lead time to prevent their attack.

Which was why Carter believed the rest of the cell had to be stopped, here and now. They wouldn't get a better chance. But the obvious presence of the feds and police searching everything was not helping. Carter walked on, looking for any sign of Hannah. She was his number one priority now, but he couldn't help but wonder if there was something else he could do to help corral the terrorist cell. If he knew who was in charge, he'd have a word with them about strategy.

"Carter? Is that you?" A woman's voice

came to Carter from one of the storefront doorways. He swiveled his head to find a familiar face there. A woman he hadn't seen in many years, but knew well. In fact, the last he'd heard, she was a high-ranking FBI agent.

"Lina?" Carter stopped walking and took off his sunglasses.

"It *is* you." Lina smiled at him and stepped closer, clearing the doorway. She had a steaming cup of coffee in her hand. "Now, if I was a suspicious sort, I'd wonder why, exactly, you—of all people—were here."

Carter thought about his response for a split second and decided to go with honesty. "What if I told you, I know what all these good people are doing, and I think they're going about it all wrong if they really want to end the threat?"

One of her eyebrows rose just a fraction. "Really?"

He nodded. "Really. I didn't get this intel only for the locals to screw it up. They've got lead time—thanks to me—and they're going to scare the targets away with this obvious display."

"So, you just came by to see what we were up to and criticize?" Lina had gotten even more cagey in the years since they'd last met, if that were possible.

"No, ma'am. I had my orders, and you'll notice I'm here as a civilian. I wouldn't *be* here if it wasn't for another civilian and her friend, who I am trying to extricate from this location with the least amount of fuss." He let a little of his frustration show and saw Lina's eyes widen in surprise.

"A woman? You're here chasing down a woman?" Lina sounded shocked.

She might well be. Carter had known all those years ago in training that Lina was attracted to him, but he'd been intent on his work and had never even asked her out. Their potential relationship had turned into a respectful friendship, and that was it. She'd probably thought he was gay or something, because Lina was a knock-out, and she had been choosey, as well. All the guys had envied him when she'd expressed an interest, and they'd teased him about his decision to *be a monk*, as they had put it.

They'd met at a special class for sharpshooters given at Quantico. It wasn't usual for there to be such a mix of students, but the instructor had been a bit of a celebrity in shooting circles, and people had come from all backgrounds of law enforcement to study with the master for a few weeks. Only the best of the best had been granted admission to the class, and Lina was the equal or better of any man in the room. Put a weapon in her hand, and she could hit just about anything from just about any distance. She had been a rare talent, and one of the star pupils of the already elite class.

Carter just nodded in reply to Lina's query. She studied him for a moment, her expression searching.

"You must really have it bad to come down here when you *know* you weren't invited," she

179

mused. "Still, it's good to know the intel was solid. So far, we haven't found anything."

"Because you started too early." He gave her a piercing look. "Are you in charge of this show?"

Lina nodded. This just got better and better. He'd fantasized about giving the leader of this op a piece of his mind. Here was his chance.

"If you'll take my advice, you'll pull back all your troops and see if you can salvage anything out of this op." He looked around, his gaze sweeping the street. "The packages weren't supposed to be delivered until the last minute."

"How do you know? It takes time to plant IEDs."

"Lina, I was the interpreter. I heard it myself," he admitted while she favored him with a narrow-eyed look.

Finally, she sighed. "Well, we've searched up and down and haven't found a thing, so your suggestion is a good one." She pulled a radio out of her pocket and began issuing orders. Carter started to walk away, but she stopped him by calling his name. "Carter, where will you be?"

"Still have to find my quarry," he reminded her. "I'm not officially here. Remember?"

Lina shook her head and smiled. "All right. Thanks for the tip. Anything else you can share before you go?"

"I'd watch village trucks. It sounded like at least one of their men was on the inside. If you see a village sanitation or landscaping truck show up, watch them very carefully and be ready to catch them in the act."

Lina nodded and gave him a lazy salute as he went on his way, still on his quest to find Hannah.

*

As luck would have it, Lina observed a pickup truck painted with the village's seal and clear identification that it was part of the grounds keeping department. It drove right through the police barricade that had been set up to keep non-official vehicles out of the parade zone. There were plants in the back, and when the groundskeeper tried to plant not only a flower in the first giant pot, but also a pipe bomb, Lina's men closed in on him.

They took him down easily and quietly. No fuss. No muss. And, most importantly, no civilians alerted to a problem. The truck was driven away quickly and quietly by a very brave bomb squad unit member and taken directly to the county's bomb disposal range, which thankfully, wasn't too far away. Once they got off the parade route, some of the squad cars peeled off and escorted the village truck swiftly on its way.

Lina looked around and wondered if that was all. The satisfaction of a successful hunt filled her, but something was missing. It felt almost...incomplete. Lina left her squad to do the cleanup and went sniffing around on foot, checking the parade route top to bottom one more time, on her own.

*

"I wonder what that van is doing there?" Hannah asked, pointing to a van marked with the village crest and the words *Water Department* on the side.

It was parked on a side street with its back doors open and a little tent obscuring the fact that it was over a manhole, and the manhole was being opened. Hannah could see under the bottom of the flimsy tent, which didn't quite reach the ground.

Hannah turned the corner onto the deserted side street and stared hard. Something definitely wasn't right with that van. Then, it came to her.

They weren't just planting bombs in the roadside planters. They were going to put them under the manhole covers too. Damn. If they got into the sewer system, they could plant anything they wanted anywhere along the route.

Hannah ran to the van and ripped away the little tent. They had the manhole cover halfway off, but she'd made one major miscalculation. There were three of them, to one of her.

"Shit."

Carter caught sight of Hannah just as she was disappearing around a corner. Her disguise was pretty good, but he knew the shape and feel of her body now, and there was no way to hide her luscious curves and elegant, athletic physique. Lulu hung back but then followed hesitantly behind Hannah. Carter swore and broke into a run.

He turned the corner just in time to see three men square off against Hannah, who had dropped back into a fighting stance. The men were laughing at her and making derogatory remarks in their own language about the feeble female who thought she could fight. What they talked about doing to her once they subdued her made Carter's blood boil.

He saw Lulu and slowed to tell her to run for help and ask for Lina Goodwell, FBI. Wisely, Lulu took off running back the way they'd come. Now, Carter just had to get Hannah out of trouble. By the time he reached the fight, they'd already started feinting against Hannah, but she was well trained and a good fighter. She could hold her own for a little while, but three against one were bad odds.

The terrorists had their backs to him, so he was able to come in with a flying kick to take down one man right away. He squared off with another while the third kept on Hannah. While the first guy lay on the ground, dazed, the odds were evened, for a bit. Carter positioned himself back to back with Hannah, and they set to work.

The enemy were skilled fighters who fought dirty. Carter was equal to the task, but he worried about Hannah. Like most people who learned martial arts, she'd likely been trained in a civilized dojo setting. He wasn't sure if she would be aware of the dirty tricks her opponent might pull. He spared a glance or two in her direction, but the man he was fighting took most of his concentration. He really was a superior fighter, which made Carter rethink the level of this terrorist cell. They had better-than-good training, and even though they'd been a sleeper cell in this country for years, they'd kept up with their skills.

The action was lively enough that Carter had lost track of the first man he'd knocked to the ground. It was only when he heard the distinct metallic sound of a hammer being cocked that he realized losing track of that guy had been a big mistake. Carter turned slightly toward the van, and there he stood. Dirty and dusty, but with a very lethal weapon in his hand, trained on Hannah.

"Give up or the girl dies," the man said in perfect English.

Carter raised his hands, keeping a wary eye on his opponent and everyone else involved.

"Let's not be too hasty here," he said, striving for calm, even though he was breathing hard from the fight.

"Get down on the ground," the gunman ordered. Carter was in a no-win situation. He knew he couldn't trust these guys. No matter what he did now, unless something drastic changed, he and Hannah were in big trouble.

Pretending to comply while hesitating as long as possible, Carter went through the motions of backing off. What he didn't realize, until the hole appeared in the gunman's forehead, was that until he'd moved, Carter had been blocking Lina's shot.

True to her past abilities, Lina drilled a hole in the gunman's head from twenty yards away. It took a moment for the man to fall, by which time, Carter had figured out what had happened, and he was re-engaged with the enemy he'd been fighting all along. Hannah, too, was fighting her man and holding her own.

Carter glanced down to the corner and saw Lina heading their way at speed. She certainly moved fast when she wanted. Something about her clicked in Carter's brain at that moment, and everything he'd experienced in the past—all those inexplicable moments in Lina's presence that he couldn't explain—suddenly made sense based on his recently-acquired knowledge.

Lina was a shifter of some kind. Had to be.

"Need some help here?" Lina asked, startling the man Carter was fighting enough that Carter was able to get in a knockout punch to the jaw. The guy spun around with the force of Carter's fist and dropped to the ground like a rock.

When Hannah's opponent saw Carter coming, he tried to run, but Lina was on him, cuffing his hands before anybody knew what was happening. Yeah. She was definitely some kind of shifter. No normal human female moved that fast, or had that much power.

Carter went back to the guy he'd knocked down and zip-tied his hands and feet before turning back to find Lina making Hannah's acquaintance. The women seemed respectful of each other. Whatever attraction Lina had felt for him years ago hadn't translated to any sort of jealousy, judging by the looks of things. Carter was glad. Lina was a nice person, in addition to being a crack shot and one of the good guys. Now that he suspected she was also a shifter, he definitely wanted to keep her friendship. After all the weirdness that had happened in his life lately, it was good to have at least one friend from his past that he might be able to be honest with.

She'd also be a good contact for the unit if they ever needed to get information out through less than official channels. Carter would have a talk with Hal about Lina when he got back to base, for sure.

"I think I stopped them before they could get down into the sewer, but it wouldn't hurt to have someone check, just to be sure," Hannah was saying to Lina when Carter joined them.

"You'll also want the bomb squad to take custody of this van," Carter said in a low voice, pointing to the interior.

"Holy crap." Lina's face paled, but anger sparked in her eyes at the pile of pipe bombs clearly visible within the back of the van.

"Those are IEDs, right?" Hannah asked, also pale and breathing a bit hard from exertion and adrenaline.

"Got it in one, Sergeant," Carter replied, subtly letting Lina know that Hannah was military. Lina looked at him and nodded once. Message received.

"Can you handle the rest of this?" Carter asked Lina point blank.

She looked around, assessing the situation.

"Yeah. I'll call my team. We'll mop this up."

"Great. Because I'm not here," Carter told her, putting on his sunglasses, which had miraculously survived the fight in his pocket unscathed. "I never was." He bent to pick up his baseball cap and dusted it off on his thigh before putting it back on. He smiled at Lina and put his arm around Hannah's shoulder. "You okay, champ?"

"I'm fine," she told him, though he knew she'd taken more than a few hits during the fight. Still, she wasn't bleeding, or limping, and she wasn't cringing too much. She'd probably be all right until they could get to Rick for a real assessment. Hannah turned to Lina and nodded. "Thanks for your timely help. I thought we were done for, but that shot was just amazing."

Lina looked down, shaking her head slightly. "Glad I made it in the nick of time. Next time, Carter, we're going to have to coordinate our moves a little better than this." She had the ghost of a smile on her face as she looked up at him.

"If there is a next time—and I feel like there probably will be, the way my life has been going lately—I'll be sure to do that. Good to see you, Lina. My C.O. will be in touch, I'm sure."

"I look forward to it," Lina answered easily.

At that moment, his cell phone rang, and he excused himself to dig it out of his pocket while Lina looked more closely inside the back of the van, and Hannah stood by, still catching her breath.

He said few words, listening closely to the short message. Hannah looked at Carter as he ended the call, and he nodded.

"That was the last of them," he announced softly. "We got them all."

Lina looked at him sharply. She'd heard his words and walked the few steps back to rejoin them.

"Good. I'm going to sit for a minute," Hannah said. "You two talk. I just want to take a breather."

"You okay?" Carter asked, immediately concerned, but Hannah waved him off as she walked a few yards away and sat on the curb.

He realized she had probably figured out there were things he might want to say to Lina in private, and she was giving him space. Hannah, once again, was showing her sensitivity. How could he not love this woman?

The L word didn't scare him. Not anymore. Not after all they'd been through and how much he'd realized his life would be empty without Hannah in it. She was the missing piece he hadn't realized he'd needed until he'd found her.

He saw Lulu come around the corner down the block at that point. She started walking toward them a bit hesitantly, but she was definitely on her way to meet them. Whatever he was going to say to Lina, he should probably say it before Lulu got within earshot.

He spared a last glance for Hannah, sitting on the curb a few yards distant. She looked okay, just a bit winded and maybe a little bit in shock. He'd take care of her, but he had to leave things on the right note with Lina first. He decided to talk fast.

"You know, I've learned a bit about the wider world since I last saw you," he said, gauging her reaction. "Have you ever heard of a Navy Commander named Kinkaid?"

"Possibly," Lina said after a moment of hesitation. Oh, yeah. She'd definitely known about Kinkaid.

The name clearly meant something to her, but she wasn't revealing much. She was cautious. He could respect that. If she really was a shifter, as he suspected, then she had every right to be wary. Her kind had managed to keep their secrets for centuries, if Kinkaid was to be believed.

"The thing is, we're stationed on his base right now. There's a reason for that," Carter went on, feeling his way. "The call I just got? That was from a seer." Lina's eyes narrowed. "That's how I know we won't have any more trouble today."

"Reliable?" Lina asked, surprising Carter with her easy acceptance of his claim.

Hot damn. She knew what he was talking about when he called Jeff a *seer*, like Kinkaid had. Carter had to be right about her. She had to be a shifter.

"I trust him with my life. He's never been wrong yet," he replied immediately and Lina nodded. "Thing is, if you ever need any...help...or special intel, you should probably talk to Commander Kinkaid. He can connect the dots between my group and anything you need to know. On home ground, you know our hands are tied. Legally, we really can't operate on U.S. soil. But that doesn't mean we stop being who and what we are. We can help, but we need to work through others, for now. We don't mind giving you the credit. We don't need accolades, just to know that we've done what we can to protect the innocent."

"Noble," Lina replied after a moment, putting a great deal of respect into the word. "I'll look up this Kinkaid and open a channel of communication. If he vouches for you, well, we'll take it from there," she promised.

She wasn't saying anything to confirm she was as he suspected, but he'd given her the contact name so she could have him checked out. Maybe, after she talked to Kinkaid, she'd be more trusting. Time would tell. For now, he was content to have laid the groundwork.

She held out her hand, and he shook it. "You were always a special guy, Carter, but I knew we weren't meant to be." Lina looked over to where Hannah was sitting. "Your lady is formidable. I'm glad you finally found your mate."

That last word struck Carter as odd. Like it had some kind of deeper meaning. Maybe it did to Lina's kind. Carter made a mental note to ask the younger, more approachable, Kinkaid about it, if he got the chance. In the meantime, Carter had to check on Hannah and get her out of here before Lina's team showed up.

He joined Hannah after saying goodbye to Lina, and they made their way down the block.

CHAPTER FOURTEEN

Hannah wasn't sure how to explain any of this to Lulu, but when they caught up to her, halfway to the corner, Lulu just reached out and pulled Hannah into a big hug. Hannah was bruised, but the hug from her overwrought best friend felt good. When Lulu backed off, she had tears in her eyes.

"I always knew you were a badass, but I've never seen you in action, Hannah. I was peeking around the corner and caught the end of the fight. You're amazing. Thank you for doing what you do and being the kind of person you are, who doesn't let bad people get away with doing bad things." She sniffed and turned to Carter, enveloping him in a surprise hug as well, while Hannah smiled at his shock. "You, too. I didn't see much, but you guys were awesome."

Lulu backed off, and Hannah made the formal introductions. "Lulu, this is Carter. He's the guy who stayed with me in the mall after that...um...incident."

"Oh, so we're back to speaking in code?" Lulu shook her head and gave Hannah a grin. "Okay, well, then. It's nice to see you again, mystery man Carter. I haven't heard all that much about you, though I do remember you taking my best friend to lunch the other day. After what I just saw, though, you should know I am duly impressed."

Carter grinned at her. "Nice to meet you officially, too, Lulu. Hannah's mentioned you more than a few times."

"So, do you think the parade will go on as planned?" Lulu asked. "My nephew has his little heart set on it. I'd hate to see him disappointed, but I also want it to be safe."

"I think we can assure you that the threat has been neutralized. Everybody should be okay from here, especially with the heightened police presence watching over everything," Carter told her as they walked around the corner and joined the light foot traffic on the street. They cleared the area just as a dark SUV—filled, no doubt, with Lina's team members—went around the corner. "The parade will go on as normal, and there shouldn't be any further problems."

"Thank God," Lulu whispered. "And thank you both, for making it happen. Things could have been a lot different here today."

"Do you want to stay and watch the parade?" Hannah asked her friend. Her bruises were starting to complain, and she wanted to get a shower as soon as possible.

"Yeah. I'm going to stay. You two go ahead. I know you probably have things to do. Reports to write. Whatever." Lulu waived her hands. "I'm going to do what I'd planned from the beginning. I'm getting myself a large coffee and sitting in the window of the coffee shop until my nephew's group marches past. Then, I'm going back to my sister's with the kid and having pizza with them for lunch."

"That sounds like a great way to spend the day," Carter told her. "We're going to walk back to my bike and get out of Dodge, if you don't mind. We have bruises to check out and, like you said, reports to make. It was nice meeting you, Lulu. I'm sure we'll see each other again in the future."

Carter offered his hand, and Lulu tugged him into another hug, but he didn't seem to mind. After letting him go, she hugged Hannah again, and then, she took herself off to that coffee shop she'd mentioned while Carter and Hannah began walking down Main Street toward wherever he'd parked.

"Who was on the phone?" Hannah asked Carter after a few minutes of walking silently.

"Jeeves. He and Rose saw what went down, and they were able to confirm we got them all," Carter told her. "It was like Rose said. If you hadn't come here today, half the cell would have gotten away with their van full of those things. Nobody was looking for that water truck or worried about the manholes, though they should have been. Heads might roll in the water department after this. They should have had someone watching for that kind of infiltration."

"Maybe the guys we fought were the ones assigned to that task," Hannah mused. "They were water department employees, after all."

"Hmm. Yeah, that's a possibility, too. There'll be a full investigation. I trust Lina to get to the bottom of it, whatever it was."

"You knew her from before?" Hannah tried not to be jealous, but then again, they hadn't given off the *former lovers* vibe to her. Maybe they'd only been friends.

"We took an elite sharpshooting class together a few years back. No need to tell you, she's one of the best shots I've ever known." Carter sounded admiring rather than attracted, if she was any judge. Good.

"Was she using a silencer? Is that why nobody heard the gunfire?" Hannah asked, not realizing until she thought about it, just now, that she hadn't heard the shot that had taken out one of the terrorists. If a gunshot had sounded anywhere near that parade route, police and others would have come running a lot sooner.

"Yeah, she had a silencer. Not sure why, except maybe she didn't want to alarm the public with the sound of open gunfire, if she could help it," Carter mused.

"Smart lady," Hannah stated.

"She's a pro," Carter said off-handedly. "And, by the way, so are you, Sergeant." He dipped close to place a quick kiss on her temple. "You were amazing. You've got moves, woman!"

She liked the teasing and pride she heard in his voice. "Thanks, and same goes for you. I was glad to have you at my back."

"Me, too. I'd have you there anytime, Hannah. You're the real deal."

As declarations went, it was an odd one, but she'd take it.

They came to a sleek Harley a few moments later, and she wasn't surprised when he reached into a back compartment and pulled out two helmets, one of which was purple with a pink stripe.

"I borrowed this from Casey, just in case," Carter said, offering the purple helmet to Hannah.

She laughed and took it, yanking off the wig she was still wearing and stuffing the lumpy thing in her pocket. Her own hair probably couldn't look much worse, so she put on the helmet, not caring that it would further squash her hair. Better safe than glamorous, she figured.

"Are we going right back to the island?" she asked.

"For now. I want Rick to look you over. I know you took some hard hits. It's just a precaution. Then, I'm going to ask the captain for some time off. If you're amenable, I'd like to spend it with you."

A slow grin spread over Hannah's face. She felt breathless and exhilarated all at once, but tried to play it cool.

"I'd like that a lot."

She was very much afraid she had just about purred, but Carter didn't seem to mind. He leaned in close for a hot kiss that stole her breath, then stepped away and donned his helmet. He got on the monster bike and waited for her to do the same. It was a moment before Hannah could get her mind working properly again. She realized she finally knew what it felt like to be kissed senseless.

She wanted to feel it again. And again. And again.

*

When they got to the island, Rick looked them both over, checking for internal damage from the fight. He spent a few moments healing contusions but otherwise pronounced them both fit.

Hannah thanked him for his ministrations. She hadn't looked forward to the sore black and blue marks she would have been sporting for a week or two without his help. As it was, he'd made it like the fight had never happened, which was still a marvel to her.

Carter and Hannah then spent an hour briefing Hal on exactly what had taken place. When they'd reached the end of their story, Hal sent Hannah off to get some dinner but kept

Carter for a while longer. When Carter failed to reappear after another hour had passed, Hannah grew concerned, but Rose kept her company and told her not to worry. Carter came into the common room a short while later, much to Hannah's relief.

"Sorry. I just had to discuss a few things with Hal and request that leave I mentioned earlier," he told her when they were alone on the sofa.

Rose left when Carter came in, smiling knowingly at them both as she walked out of the common room. A few of the other guys were across the room, playing chess, but they were engrossed in the game and weren't paying any real attention to Carter and Hannah.

"He's given me time off, starting tomorrow, but he wants us both to stay on base tonight," Carter told her. "There might be a unit meeting in the morning that I'll have to be at. Sorry."

"Don't be sorry. It's all good," she told him, and she meant it. Being with him wasn't just good. It was the very best. No matter where they were.

When they retreated to the privacy of his room later that night, they weren't in a hurry, unlike the other times they'd been together. No, finally, they were able to savor their moments together, undressing each other with long, leisurely strokes of fingers and hands, and lips and mouths.

Hannah was panting by the time Carter had done away with the last item of clothing separating them. Her knees were so weak that she was glad when he picked her up and carried her over to the bed. She wasn't exactly sure if she would have made it on her own.

He started by laying her down on the bed and kissing her all over. All over. Hannah squirmed under his ministrations, biting her tongue to keep from screaming in pleasure at various points in the seductive torture of his hands and tongue. He questioned her throughout, with words and body language, learning what she liked, what she loved, and what made her giddy in the best possible way.

But she wasn't going to let him do all the work. When she'd come down from a small climax that made her see stars, she pushed at his shoulders until he rolled over in supplication. Flat on his back, his long legs draped over the side of the bed, she gave him the same treatment, starting with her hands and ending with her tongue, kissing and nibbling on any, and every, part of his muscular body that struck her fancy.

He remained stoic throughout, growling low in his throat but not allowing any louder sound to make it past his lips. He didn't want them to become the talk of the barracks. It was fun, in a way, to have to hold back on the noise. It made the interlude somehow naughtier. More of a secret shared between the two of them, though she had little doubt in her rational mind that everyone knew they were a couple now. Still, being together, on base, still held a hint of the forbidden, because on any *regular* base, fraternization like this would have been strictly *verboten.*

She was enjoying herself, licking him like a popsicle, when he seemed to snap out of it. He rose, and with strong, competent hands, he lifted her into place, putting her exactly where he wanted her. In this case, she ended up on her hands and knees in the middle of the bed, her ass up in the air as he took up a position behind her. He took his time, gathering her loose hair in one hand and placing nibbling, exciting love bites on her neck before he did anything else.

"You okay with this?" he asked, his voice a growl near her ear, which he promptly nibbled on, in turn.

"Okay?" She could barely find the breath to reply. Her senses were spinning, and Carter was a grand master at keeping her on the edge of stupefied wonder. "I'm okay," she gasped, wanting him to get on with it already. "Do it now," she begged. "Please."

Boy, did she sound pitiful, or what? Next time, she'd turn the tables on him, but for now, she was too busy enjoying being in this very compromising position with the man of her dreams.

Mercifully, Carter didn't make her wait. His rumbling chuckle sounded as he took up his position behind her and pushed home. Thus began a long, languid rocking motion that drove her higher and higher still, all the while withholding the final prize. The ultimate dream. The brilliant star he was pushing her toward.

She was so close to screaming out her

feelings toward him, but that wouldn't be romantic at all. Plus, she kind of wanted to hear more about his feelings before she blurted out her own. Besides, who could think when she was so close to nirvana?

So, instead of telling him how much she loved every last thing about him, she just grit her teeth and begged him to go faster, harder, deeper...anything that would end this intense longing for completion. Anything that would give her the deep satisfaction and luminous pleasure she had only ever found with him. Carter. Her knight in shining armor who let her be her own woman in a way few men ever had.

She admired him. She enjoyed being with him. Most of all, she liked who she was when she was with him. Who he encouraged her to be. Everything that was inside of her. All the things she'd been afraid to show others. She let it all come out with Carter, and he hadn't run in the other direction. Far from it.

He'd given her encouragement and approval. Praise and, oh, so much pleasure. He'd protected her—more than once—but he'd also let her be who she was and respected that she could do many things and didn't always need, or want, to be the damsel in distress.

The times he'd protected her, he'd done so without making a big deal of it. He'd done it quietly, before she even became aware of it. He'd shown himself to be a man of honor who respected her on every level. She loved that about him, and so much more.

She reached back blindly, urging him on, and

he gave her what she wanted. Her throat was raw with holding back the shrieks of passion as he drove her higher and higher still, until finally, they crested the wave together and surfed the sensations that shot them both to the stars...and beyond.

*

The next morning, Carter and Hannah made their escape from the island for a few days off. They stopped at a grocery and a hardware store before going to her place. She put the groceries away and cleared out the fridge of anything that had gotten too old while she'd been busy elsewhere, while he tackled the bugs and cameras that the enemy had put in place.

Carter felt great satisfaction in ripping out the surveillance. He also carefully removed her system and put it aside for later discussion. He wanted her to have security in her home, but maybe not cameras pointing inside, just in case the WiFi feed got hijacked in future. There were other ways, and other bits of equipment he'd rather see in place, but he'd talk it all over with Hannah first. It was her home, after all.

Although, if things went the way he hoped they would, he might be spending a lot more time with her. Today was the day. He was going to tell her how he felt and find out if she felt even a glimmer of the same way about him. He was more than a little nervous about it, if he was being honest with himself.

He may have spent a little more time than was absolutely necessary taking down the cameras and microphones. By the time he was done, Hannah had lunch on the table, waiting for him.

"I'm not usually this domestic," she explained when he walked into the kitchen and found her waiting with food on the table. "This is just a thank you for taking care of my little bug problem."

Carter hefted the cardboard box full of equipment he'd removed from all over her home. "Not so little, as it turned out."

Her eyes widened. "All that was in my house?"

"Yeah. This is in addition to the system you bought. I left those pieces in the living room," he told her. "I wanted to discuss redeployment of those pieces in a more effective pattern."

"You didn't just do it?" She seemed surprised.

"I wouldn't put a system in place without your input. It's your home, Hannah. I want you to feel safe here."

Her expression softened as he spoke, and he knew he'd made the right decision. For about two seconds after he took out the first component, he thought about just reinstalling it in a better location, but he'd decided rather quickly that wasn't the way to go. In this case, his instincts had been right.

"Thanks," she said, moving forward to put her arms around his waist and hug him close.

She'd been through so much lately, it felt

good to just stop for a moment and share the closeness of each other's presence.

"You know..." He spoke in a low voice, near her ear. "You took a few years off my life by running away from the island and smack into danger."

"I'm sorry. I was just so frustrated that nobody was doing anything," she replied, nestling her head into his shoulder.

"Honey, you should have trusted me. Trusted the unit. We would never have let anything really bad happen, if we could stop it. In fact, it was Rose and Jeff that told me I had to let you go so that the threat could be completely dealt with," he revealed.

"They did?" She lifted her head to meet his gaze.

"Give me some credit. I knew you were leaving almost before you did. Jeff held me back while Rose helped you go. It nearly killed me, but I listened and let it happen." He took a deep breath and went on, taking a massive risk. "I love you, but don't ever do that to me again, okay?"

Hannah felt her heart skip a beat. Had he really said what she'd thought he said?

"You love me?" Hope made her dizzy. Good thing she had him to cling to for support.

Carter nodded. "I do. I have for a while, but I wasn't sure how you'd react if I told you about my feelings. Are you okay with it?"

"Okay?" She wasn't sure what to say. Words nearly failed her. "I'm... I'm floored."

"In a good way, I hope?" He seemed unsure so she raised one hand to cup his cheek, hoping to make herself understood.

"In the best possible way," she told him. "I can't believe how fast I've fallen in love with you," she went on, finding words, though it was still hard. "Or how hard I fell. I desperately want to see where this all leads. With you."

"That's good," Carter told her, a grin spreading across his handsome face. "Because I have some very definite ideas about sharing happily ever after with you, Hannah. In fact, I already asked Hal to put in a request, seeing if maybe we could get you reassigned to the island base, so we can be together and work together."

"Fraternization?" She gave him a teasing smile. "I don't believe that's allowed, Sergeant."

"You may have noticed, we sort of make up our own rules since the desert, and for the most part, the Army lets us. It's definitely an odd situation, so we should take full advantage of it while it lasts." His gaze narrowed. "That's assuming my instincts are right, and you want to be back in the Army and back on active duty. Did I get that part right?"

"You did. I didn't like the way my career almost ended. I want to go out—if I leave the service anytime soon—on my own terms. Not because of a disability. For now, I'd be honored to work with your unit, if they'll have me." She couldn't believe what he had already arranged.

"They all think it's great. I sort of asked them about it last night," he admitted.

"You did?" This just got better and better.

"There's just one more thing I want to ask you about," he said, his voice dropping low as he stepped back, releasing her from his embrace but keeping hold of her hands.

He dropped to one knee, and her mouth went dry with shock. He looked up at her, and she really thought she could see their future unfolding before her, in the intense blue of his eyes.

"Will you do me the honor of becoming my wife?" He asked her the words she had never quite believed she'd hear from him.

She squeezed his hands as a tear rolled down her face. A tear of pure, distilled joy.

There was only one answer she could give as her heart opened and filled with the wonder of this moment and all the years they could have together. She searched her heart and found the answer, giving it to him with a single word...

"Yes."

EPILOGUE

Meanwhile on Plum Island...

Lina was shown into Commander Kinkaid's office by some kind of sea-based shifter she had never encountered before. She'd scented a few werewolves manning the guard post, but other than them, this place smelled like a lot of big cats. Really big cats.

She'd met jaguars before, but never lions. And the Kinkaid Clan was reputed to be chock full of lions and selkies. If this commander was part of the Kinkaid Clan—and chances were astoundingly good that he was—then it made sense that he might just be one of those fierce lion shifters that most Others both feared and envied.

The man behind the desk stood and offered

a hand when she walked in. He had sandy blond hair and piercing blue eyes that seemed to see right through her. Lina marshalled her courage and took the man's hand, returning the very human gesture of greeting.

"Thank you for accepting my invitation to visit the base," he said, smiling. "I'm Lester Kinkaid." It went without saying that he was the Alpha in charge of every shifter on this island. Dominance came off the guy in waves.

"Lina Goodwell, as you know," she replied, keeping her tone friendly. They were both feeling each other out.

"I've heard good things about you from Sergeant Carter, and you should know, I've read your file. The classified one," he told her. "Very impressive, even for one of our kind."

"Thank you, Alpha," she replied, giving him the respect of one shifter for a more dominant leader.

"The only thing the classified file doesn't tell me—and something I thought I might be able to discern by meeting you but haven't figured out yet—is exactly what kind of shifter you are." He tilted his head to the side, as if in slight embarrassment. "Forgive the rude question, but if we're going to work together, I'd like to know. If it helps, I'm a lion, as you've probably guessed from my last name."

"I suspected," Lina replied, playing for time. "I assume you're in the line of succession to the lion throne?"

Kinkaid started and shook his head. "No, not me. I'm the king's uncle, but I don't carry the marker to be king. I'm not a white lion."

"Forgive me. I didn't know your folk had the same sort of system as the tigers, where the Goddess marks those fit to rule with white fur." She was intrigued by the thought. "My kind follow the Lords. We don't have monarchs within our own species." She cleared her throat. "Uh, I'm a lynx, sir."

Kinkaid smiled with genuine warmth. "A cat. That's great. I hate to say it, but the few wolves on this base confound me. I really don't understand their Pack instincts, but please don't tell anyone I said so. They're good men and women. The fault isn't with them, but with my limited understanding of their inner beasts."

And it took a big man to admit that, Lina realized. She could definitely work with this lion. She'd been afraid he'd be an unreasonable fellow, but this man reminded her a lot of her own father. Smart, steady, and strong in dominance, but not a jerk about it. She smiled at him.

"Nobody will ever hear it from me," she told him. "Though, I happen to agree with you. Wolves are just weird. All that howling is enough to drive a lynx to drink." She shook her head, and he chuckled, as she'd hoped he would.

And thus, she thought, was the start of what might be a very good working relationship. This man was one of the good ones, and she had long ago pledged her energy toward protecting the innocent, catching bad guys, enforcing the will of the Goddess, and serving Her Light.

"Let me tell you a bit about your friend, Carter, and his unit. This, of course, is strictly need-to-know, so it can't go beyond these walls. However, if you're going to be one of their points of contact, you need to know there's more to them than just being highly-decorated Green Berets. They started out human enough, but they had a magical encounter that's changed them, and what's most important for you to know is that they all—whether they call it that or not—serve the Light."

That was music to her ears. Anything that would help her do her job and fulfill her self-appointed mission was all to the good, as far as she was concerned. She leaned forward in her seat, her gaze narrowing as she listened intently.

"Tell me more…"

# # #

ABOUT THE AUTHOR

Bianca D'Arc has run a laboratory, climbed the corporate ladder in the shark-infested streets of lower Manhattan, studied and taught martial arts, and earned the right to put a whole bunch of letters after her name, but she's always enjoyed writing more than any of her other pursuits. She grew up and still lives on Long Island, where she keeps busy with an extensive garden, several aquariums full of very demanding fish, and writing her favorite genres of paranormal, fantasy and sci-fi romance.

Bianca loves to hear from readers and can be reached through Twitter (@BiancaDArc), Facebook (BiancaDArcAuthor) or through the various links on her website.

WELCOME TO THE D'ARC SIDE... WWW.BIANCADARC.COM

OTHER BOOKS BY BIANCA D'ARC

**Brotherhood
of Blood**
One & Only
Rare Vintage
Phantom Desires
Sweeter Than Wine
Forever Valentine
Wolf Hills*
Wolf Quest

Tales of the Were
Lords of the Were
Inferno

The Others
Rocky
Slade

String of Fate
Cat's Cradle
King's Throne
Jacob's Ladder
Her Warriors

Redstone Clan
The Purrfect Stranger
Grif
Red
Magnus
Bobcat
Matt

Gifts of the Ancients
Warrior's Heart
Future Past
A Friend in Need

Grizzly Cove
All About the Bear
Mating Dance
Night Shift
Alpha Bear
Saving Grace
Bearliest Catch
The Bear's Healing Touch
The Luck of the Shifters
Badass Bear
Loaded for Bear
Bounty Hunter Bear
Storm Bear
Bear Meets Girl
Spirit Bear
Lion in Waiting
Black Magic Bear

Were-Fey Trilogy
Lone Wolf
Snow Magic
Midnight Kiss

Lick of Fire Trilogy
Phoenix Rising
Phoenix and the Wolf
Phoenix and the Dragon

Jaguar Island (Howls)
The Jaguar Tycoon
The Jaguar Bodyguard
The Jaguar's Secret Baby

Big Wolf
A Touch of Class

* RT Book Reviews Awards
Nominee
** EPPIE Award Winner
*** CAPA Award Winner

LONE WOLF

Josh is a werewolf who suddenly has extra, unexpected and totally untrained powers. He's not happy about it - or about the evil jackasses who keep attacking him, trying to steal his magic. Forced to seek help, Josh is sent to an unexpected ally for training.

Deena is a priestess with more than her share of magical power and a unique ability that has made her a target. She welcomes Josh, seeing a kindred soul in the lone werewolf. She knows she can help him... if they can survive their enemies long enough.

SNOW MAGIC

Evie has been a lone wolf since the disappearance of her mate, Sir Rayburne, a fey knight from another realm. Left all alone with a young son to raise, Evie has become stronger than she ever was. But now her son is grown and suddenly Ray is back.

Ray never meant to leave Evie all those years ago but he's been caught in a magical trap, slowly being drained of magic all this time. Freed at last, he whisks Evie to the only place he knows in the mortal realm where they were happy and safe—the rustic cabin in the midst of a North Dakota winter where they had been newlyweds. He's used the last of his magic to get there and until he recovers a bit, they're stuck in the middle of nowhere with a blizzard coming and bad guys on their trail.

Can they pick up where they left off and rekindle the magic between them, or has it been extinguished forever?

MIDNIGHT KISS

Margo is a werewolf on a mission...with a disruptively handsome mage named Gabe. She can't figure out where Gabe fits in the pecking order, but it doesn't seem to matter to the attraction driving her wild. Gabe knows he's going to have to prove himself in order to win Margo's heart. He wants her for his mate, but can she give her heart to a mage? And will their dangerous quest get in the way?

PHOENIX RISING

Lance is inexplicably drawn to the sun and doesn't understand why. Tina is a witch who remembers him from their high school days. She'd had a crush on the quiet boy who had an air of magic about him. Reunited by Fate, she wonders if she could be the one to ground him and make him want to stay even after the fire within him claims his soul...if only their love can be strong enough.

PHOENIX AND THE WOLF

Diana is drawn to the sun and dreams of flying, but her elderly grandmother needs her feet firmly on the ground. When Diana's old clunker breaks down in front of a high-end car lot, she seeks help and finds herself ensnared by the sexy werewolf mechanic who runs the repair shop. Stone makes her want to forget all her responsibilities and take a walk on the wild side...with him.

PHOENIX AND THE DRAGON

He's a dragon shapeshifter in search of others like himself. She's a newly transformed phoenix shifter with a lot to learn and bad guys on her trail. Together, they will go on a dazzling adventure into the unknown, and fight against evil folk intent on subduing her immense power and using it for their own ends. They will face untold danger and find love that will last a lifetime.

THE JAGUAR TYCOON

Mark may be the larger-than-life billionaire Alpha of the secretive Jaguar Clan, but he's a pussycat when it comes to the one women destined to be his mate. Shelly is an up-and-coming architect trying to drum up business at an elite dinner party at which Mark is the guest of honor. When shots ring out, the hunt for the gunman brings Mark into Shelly's path and their lives will never be the same.

THE JAGUAR BODYGUARD

Sworn to protect his Clan, Nick heads to Hollywood to keep an eye on a rising star who has seen a little too much for her own good. Unexpectedly fame has made a circus of Sal's life, but when decapitated squirrels show up on her doorstep, she knows she needs professional help. Nick embeds himself in her security squad to keep an eye on her as sparks fly and passions rise between them. Can he keep her safe and prevent her from revealing what she knows?

THE JAGUAR'S SECRET BABY

Hank has never forgotten the wild woman with whom he spent one memorable night. He's dreamed of her for years now, but has never been back to the small airport in Texas owned and run by her werewolf Pack. Tracy was left with a delicious memory of her night in Hank's arms, and a beautiful baby girl who is the light of her life. She chose not to tell Hank about his daughter, but when he finally returns and he discovers the daughter he's never known, he'll do all he can to set things right.

DRAGON KNIGHTS

Two dragons, two knights, and one woman to complete their circle. That's the recipe for happiness in the land of fighting dragons. But there are a few special dragons that are more. They are the ruling family and they are half-dragon and half-human, able to change at will from one form to another.

Books in this series have won the EPPIE Award for Best Erotic Romance in the Fantasy/Paranormal category, and have been nominated for RT Book Reviews Magazine Reviewers Choice Awards among other honors.

WWW.BIANCADARC.COM

Made in the USA
Coppell, TX
05 July 2021

58572400R00135